D0733825

Books by Kenneth Oppel

Sunwing
Silverwing
Dead Water Zone

(For Younger Readers)
Peg and the Whale
Emma's Emu
Follow That Star
A Bad Case of Ghosts
A Strange Case of Magic
A Crazy Case of Robots

(For Adults)
The Devil's Cure

The Live-Forever
Machine

Kenneth Oppel

The Live-Forever Machine

HarperCollins*PublishersLtd*

The Live-Forever Machine
Copyright © 1990 by Kenneth Oppel.
All rights reserved. No part of this book
may be used or reproduced in any
manner whatsoever without prior written
permission except in the case of brief
quotations embodied in reviews. For
information address
HarperCollins Publishers Ltd,
55 Avenue Road, Suite 2900,
Toronto, Ontario, Canada M5R 3L2

www.harpercanada.com

HarperCollins books may be purchased
for educational, business, or sales promo-
tional use. For information please write:
Special Markets Department,
HarperCollins Canada,
55 Avenue Road, Suite 2900,
Toronto, Ontario, Canada M5R 3L2

First published by Kids Can Press: 1990
First HarperCollins edition

Canadian Cataloguing in Publication Data

Oppel, Kenneth
The live-forever machine

I S B N 0-00-648559-6

I. Title.

PS8579.P64L5 2001   jC813'.54
C00-932367-8
PZ7.O614Li 2001

01 02 03 04 HC 4 3

Printed and bound in the United States
Set in Meridien

This book is for my mother and father

Acknowledgements

I would like to thank the Ontario Arts Council and the Canada Council for their financial assistance while I was writing this book. There are also many people who helped me put this book together one way or another: Bill MacGregor, Dylan Reid, Diana Patterson, JoAnna Dutka, Chris Torbay, Philippa Sheppard, and Charis Wahl, whose criticism was invaluable.

1

Heatwave City

Any hotter and the whole city would go up in flames.

Eric pushed the hair back from his damp forehead, waiting for an opening in the traffic. *Come on, come on.* He looked across the road to the museum. Air-conditioned: he moved the word between his lips, drawn out long and soft, like a whisper of cool wind. Good thing they lived just across the road. This was the fifth day in a row now that he'd sought refuge in the city museum. It was a lot better than hanging around in some underground mall.

He darted out, dancing around car bumpers, shuffling back from the yellow line as a convertible slung by, then running all out across the final stretch of scalding asphalt. He paused on the other side to catch his breath. The heat was like a lead apron over his narrow shoulders and chest. He could even taste the heat—damp, tinged with the sharp chemical tang of car exhaust. This stuff was poisonous.

The smothering heatwave had slouched into the city a week ago, settling over the streets like a cantankerous cat. It warped Eric's paperback books, made the walls of his paper models sag, brought his posters curling off the walls. At night the heat padded stealthily through his open window and curled up on his chest as he slept. He woke every morning in a film of sweat.

During the day the heat pooled like water on the asphalt, sending up mirages. Eric had heard news reports of drivers who had swerved to avoid nonexistent stands of trees, herds of water buffalo, and, once, an oncoming freight train.

And all across the city, things had been happening. Like the traffic lights at the intersection all flashing green for an entire morning, or the city hall bells chiming noon at four in the morning. And just yesterday, walking back from the twenty-four-hour doughnut store, he'd seen a huge column of thick black smoke explode from a manhole cover in the middle of the road.

There were stranger things, too. He'd watched from his window as all the lights in a block of downtown highrises flickered, faded, and then flared up brighter than before. In the sky, the advertising blimps, usually so slow and careful, were darting erratically like agitated beetles. They skimmed past one another, diving so low over the high peaks of the city that Eric thought they were going to crash. A few days ago, during rush hour, he'd seen a car veer off the road and slam a fire hydrant over. But there wasn't any water, just a harsh sound of sucking air. He'd heard stories of men and women sprawled in the cracked basins of dried-up fountains, begging for rain in their sleep. The newspapers had carried front-page photos of a man who'd scaled the side of a skyscraper, hoping for a cool breeze that wasn't there.

"Heatwave city," Eric muttered. It sounded like the title of one of his father's stories.

The revolving door swung him into the sudden cool of the museum. He exhaled in relief. The quiet here in the entrance hallway seemed impossible after the roar of the street. The muffled sounds of footsteps and lowered voices dissolved within the enormous space, drawn upwards like currents of air towards the high ceiling. Eric felt as if he were in a church. Light glanced softly off the smooth surface of the floor, illuminating a large circular mosaic of

2

the sun and planets in the centre of the hall. A broad staircase curved upwards to the next level and, on all sides, high corridors receded into the vastness of the museum. He breathed in the familiar smell—he'd never quite been able to nail it down. What was it? Light and dust and wood and polished stone. Did stone have a smell? It was all the smell of the past to him.

The sweat on his forehead and back cooled. He checked his pocket for the museum notebook. Every time he came, he wrote down two things that he wanted to remember. Then, during the following week, he'd memorize them. Two a visit, he'd found, was the limit—any more and he'd just forget. He'd had this particular notebook for almost three years.

He made his way towards the staircase, glancing in at the gift shop as he passed. As always, it was packed. There were probably more people in the shop than in the rest of the museum. He'd once seen a whole busload of people come through the main doors and head straight for the gift shop, buying postcards, key chains, bookmarks, placemats, coffee mugs, miniature replicas of statues they hadn't even seen. Then back they shuffled into the bus like a crowd of penguins. What was the point?

He moved through the museum, guided by the familiarity of years of visits with his father. He sometimes felt he'd grown up in the high, quiet galleries and long corridors. When he was younger, there had been trips to the zoo, the amusement park, and the library, as well, but the visits to the museum remained the strongest memories. And over the past five days, he'd spent so much time here that he'd started to dream about the museum, navigating maze-like corridors, wandering through immense galleries without ceilings, propping up sagging walls with his shoulders.

He walked quickly past display cases filled with shards of prehistoric pottery. His father would have stopped to inspect them carefully, reading every sign. If it was old, he wanted to know about it. But Eric never had the patience. He liked the big things: the Spanish galleon you could walk through, the Chinese tomb with its stone soldiers and camels, the recreated coal mine, the dinosaurs.

He paused in the corridor. His nostrils quivered. A strange, dark smell had passed through the air and he seemed to have caught the tail end of it. It wasn't a museum smell, but it wasn't unfamiliar either: it was the stale smell of oil and electricity that his father sometimes brought home with him after a long day working on the subway. Strange that it was here, though. He sniffed the air a few more times, but it was fading now, almost gone. He headed for the dinosaur gallery.

A woolly mammoth, tusks raised high in the air, stood at the entrance. He'd walked through the darkened dinosaur gallery countless times with his father: it had always been their favourite part. When Eric was younger, his father would read him the information about each dinosaur from the sign. He'd often make up a few details, though Eric hadn't known this until he got older and could read the signs for himself. "The Tyrannosaurus Rex," his father would tell him, "had such bad breath he was shunned by all the other dinosaurs and forced to live alone in the forest" or "The Brontosaurus' tail was so long that he was forever tripping over it, much to the amusement of the other dinosaurs."

The gallery was empty except for a man in black jeans and T-shirt who was just leaving. Eric reached across the railing and touched one of the dinosaur bones, encircling it with his hand: hard, varnished bone, cool to the touch.

4

Doing this wasn't strictly allowed, but what did it matter? He was being careful. There should be more things to touch in the museum anyway; somehow things seem less real when they're on the other side of a glass panel. But he knew the displays had to be protected. He could still see the initials someone had carved into the ribs of the Triceratops, and there were sometimes cigarette butts in the foliage.

He remembered his father, a few years back, wrapping his fingers around one of the dinosaur bones, and smiling, saying, "This is the way you should hold onto the past. With all your strength."

Dad was like that a lot, talking like one of the characters in his stories—and they were pretty damn hard to figure out. *With all your strength.* All right. He could understand that, maybe, if it meant trying to protect old things from getting carved up by some idiot with a jackknife. But it was never that simple with his father.

Upstairs, he stepped through the archway into the medieval gallery. On either side of the broad, dimly lit passage were magnificent displays of soldiers from the Middle Ages, some in armour, some on horseback with lances, others on foot, carrying swords or bows. Behind the railings, the displays seemed to stretch back forever across a rocky plain, into deep shadow.

He walked slowly to the end of the gallery, then started back again. He had pulled the notebook from his jeans pocket and begun to write down a description of the soldiers' armour when someone brushed past him, jostling his pencil.

"Idiot," Eric muttered, looking up.

It was the man he'd seen in the dinosaur gallery, the one dressed all in black. He was walking quickly, his shoes making a staccato click against the polished floor. And there it was again, that odour, stronger now in the man's wake. Oil and electricity. At the far end of the corridor, he stopped abruptly, silhouetted in the high archway.

Eric squinted. A second man had appeared, as if from the display, amid the horses and soldiers. Funny, he hadn't noticed anyone there when he passed a few minutes ago. The new arrival was tall and slightly stooped, dressed in coveralls. Eric caught a glimpse of silver hair and an aged, aquiline profile. The figure moved towards the archway until the two men were quite close, blackened against the light, facing each other, stock-still.

Eric watched them from the corner of his eye. There was something strange about all this. Who were these two guys? The one in coveralls looked as if he worked here. But somehow this didn't look like just a casual meeting. They stared at each other for a long time, and then the taller one took a small step forward. For a second, Eric thought he was going to embrace the one in black—long-lost friends, brothers? Instead, they began to speak, fragments of their conversation diffusing through the long corridor.

"... took me a while to catch up with you, Alexander." Who was that? Eric peered at their faces: it was the man in the black jeans talking. So the other guy, the tall guy, was Alexander.

"... most miraculous," he heard Alexander say in a low, hoarse voice. "Your hair, the colour and length of it: that is the sole difference. Otherwise, not a single alteration ... don't know why it ought to surprise me, and yet it always does. How many years ..." His voice trailed off.

Eric strained to catch the words, but they faded out like a ghost radio signal. He was too far away. He took a deep breath and stepped across the railing and into the shadows of the display. Gravel and packed dirt whispered beneath his feet. Slowly, carefully, he began moving deeper into the display, towards the two men at the far end of the gallery. The thick smell of oil made his nostrils tingle. Harsh laughter shimmered down the hallway.

"By the way, that's not my name anymore ... I've got a brand new one now." It was the man in black again. What did he mean? Eric wondered. He's changed his name? Is that it? The man said something else, but it was only an inaudible, serpentine whisper.

"... made an apt choice," Alexander replied. And then he coughed—a dry, rasping cough that jerked him forward a little.

"... not still sick, are you?" The man in black. There was a mean edge to his voice, as if he were some snickering, smart-ass kid. "Just can't shake it, can you?"

Still moving through the display, Eric bumped against one of the soldiers. He froze, holding his breath. It was all right; no one had heard. He crouched down, balanced on the balls of his feet. His jeans tightened uncomfortably around his knees. Through the legs of horses and soldiers, he watched the two men.

"You reek of machinery," Alexander said disdainfully. There was something strange about his voice, Eric noticed. Not really an accent—or not one Eric could put his finger on, anyway. Still, it was somehow foreign, maybe like a whole bunch of accents laid one on top of another.

"You got it," said the other man. "I've been busy. You look old, Alexander, very old. Aren't you getting tired of it all?"

Eric still couldn't make out his face. Turn around a little so I can see you, Mr. Dressed-in-Black.

"It was scarcely a surprise, of course," Alexander was

saying. "I was certain it was you. You proclaim your presence in unmistakable fashion: the belligerent and odious bellowing of a vandal."

Eric shook his head. This was getting very weird. He hadn't ever heard anyone talk like that, except his father when he was reading from an old book. Who *were* these guys?

"It was so easy, these last two," said the man in the black jeans as he began walking deeper into the gallery, with Alexander following a few steps behind. "Flames are best for old things, aren't they? They burn so easily. They didn't have what I was looking for, so ..."

Eric pivoted slowly on his heels, keeping the two men in view. He caught a good glimpse of the one in black. Pretty ordinary, he thought: nondescript features and short, dark hair, cropped close at the sides. Nothing special. Could have been anyone.

"... maybe you're next, Alexander. Thought about it?"

Alexander said something that Eric didn't understand. He'd never heard anything like it, a harsh clashing of consonants.

"Stop!" the man in black said harshly, and Eric thought there was panic in his voice. Then, more calmly, he said, "In English now, old man."

"Have you forgotten the others so soon?" Alexander inquired with a hint of mockery.

"There's nothing to forget."

"All of them, then. It is unthinkable to me. Even Latin?"

Latin? No one spoke Latin.

The other man said nothing. His face, Eric noticed, had the hardened, sculpted look of a mask.

"Why do you insist on returning?" Alexander asked tiredly. "Is there no remorse in you for the irreparable damage you've done over the years?"

What the hell were they talking about? Eric raged silently. He waited impatiently for them to say more, but a small cluster of visitors had come into the gallery and the two men fell silent. The visitors took a perfunctory look around, and one of them shot off what sounded like a whole roll of film without stopping. In a few minutes they were gone.

Eric fanned his hands out on the gravel to keep himself from tipping over. His long, skinny legs were beginning to ache and the right knee of his jeans had finally ripped open. Stupid pointy knees, he thought.

The two men had stopped almost directly in front of Eric. The one in black looked around as if noticing the display for the first time.

"This is very nice," he commented. "You've been working hard."

He stepped over the railing on the opposite side of the passageway and walked lazily to a soldier in chain-link armour who stood with sword and shield raised for combat.

"It's only a matter of time, old man, and time, as they say, is on my side, yes it is ..." He moved his hand carelessly over the intricate tracery on the shield, then flicked it disdainfully with his fingernail. "Very nice." He tapped the soldier's plaster face with his knuckles.

Who did this guy think he was? To just walk into the display and start poking at old, valuable things as if they were junk.

Without looking at Alexander, the man in black said, "Why don't you just give it to me?"

"No." Alexander stepped over the railing now as well.

The younger man pushed almost playfully against the soldier with his hand. It rocked slightly. Eric could feel his heart quickening in anger. Why wasn't the other guy doing anything to stop him? Why didn't he call for one of the security guards?

"I'll make you an offer you can't refuse, Alexander." Pushing against the soldier, rocking it back and forth.

"Leave now."

The soldier teetered over and went crashing to the ground. Eric almost cried out, but bottled it up before he gave himself away. His heart clattered in his chest. A huge crack had opened in the soldier's neck, and the sword and shield had been wrenched out of his broken fingers.

The man in the dark outfit turned to face Alexander. Eric couldn't look away. He felt as if he were watching some kind of hypnotic shadow play. Then, with a suddenness that made his breath snag in his throat, the two men came crashing together, arms lashing out, each one's hands straining for the other's throat. They were locked together for three, four, five seconds before they broke, moving apart, dark shapes heaving for air. Then they were back in their fighters' embrace, fighting almost silently except for the shuffle of their shoes against the floor and the whisper of clothing against clothing.

Something quite small fell out of Alexander's pocket, and Eric could have sworn he heard it land—as if every other noise in the room had been blocked out, leaving only the single, amplified sound of the object hitting the gravel. And then his eyes were pulled back to the two men. Alexander doesn't have a chance, he thought.

But then they pushed away from each other and stood at arm's length, panting.

"... forgotten how much I hated you," the younger man whispered in contempt, his breath ragged with exertion.

"Of course you did." Alexander snapped bitterly. "This is not surprising to me in the least. You forget everything."

The man in the black jeans suddenly whirled around and seized the sword from beside the toppled soldier.

Eric began to rise. This guy was crazy! But Alexander was standing still—wasn't he even afraid? What was wrong with him? Run! Eric wanted to shout.

"Useless," snapped the tall, stooped man. "Have you forgotten that too? In any event, you doubtless do not recollect how to use it." He coughed again, a violent rattling deep in his chest. One hand went out to the railing for support.

"It's here somewhere," the other man whispered viciously. "Any hiding place, I'll find. And, Alexander, there are machines—real machines that have to be seen to be believed. You can't imagine the power of them. They're beautiful. When I walked out of the Louvre that day, everything else ... before ... all a dark dream. These machines are the power and the glory, the way of the future, Alexander. You can't stop them. This is my time. Yours is over."

"Go, go," said Alexander, his voice a tired croak.

The man in black threw the sword to the ground and turned.

"The way of the future," he said again. Without looking back, he stepped over the railing and walked out of the gallery.

Eric watched as Alexander stooped over the toppled soldier and tried to stand it upright. But it was apparently too heavy and he lowered it gently to the ground. He picked up the sword and shield and examined them carefully. Then he stood up, looking around the armoury. He seemed alert, as if he were listening.

Eric pressed his hands hard against the ground and tried to remain absolutely motionless. A trickle of sweat ran down over his ribs. Whatever that was, he told himself, you were not supposed to see it.

Alexander stood a moment longer, his head tilted attentively. Then, holding the sword and the shield, he turned and moved deeper in the display, further and further back. Eric squinted after him. Where was he going? The shadows closed around him and he was soon just a dark outline, and then, nothing at all. He'd disappeared. Must be a door back there somewhere.

Eric let out a deep breath. All he wanted to do was get out, fast, but he made himself wait a few more seconds before painfully pushing himself out of his crouch. He walked quickly to the railing and hopped over onto the tiled floor. Then he hesitated. There. It was still there, just at the edge of the display.

He took one quick look around the gallery and then bent down and reached out his hand. His fingers closed around it.

2

Dad

He held it delicately in his trembling hands, as though it might disintegrate. It was an oblong of dark-grained wood, about the size and weight of a micro-cassette tape, though much thinner. Even though he was alone in the house, he had closed the bedroom door, and he sat on the edge of his bed, his heart still racing, his mouth dry.

What was it? He ran his thumb softly around the bevelled corners. It was old. He could tell. It *felt* old. There was a hinge along one of the longer sides, and he put his finger-nail between the two paper-thin halves and carefully prised them apart.

It opened like a book. His breath caught in his throat. On the right side was a tiny oil portrait of a woman. She sat in profile in front of a large open window, and in the painstakingly detailed background were a series of rolling meadows, the church spires of a town, and beyond that, the ocean, extending to the horizon.

But it was the woman's face that held his attention. Her dark eyes seemed to crackle in the painted light. She looked almost fierce, with her heavy eyebrows, strong, straight nose, and mane of reddish-brown hair brushed back in thick waves from her high forehead. But her full mouth was vulnerable and gentle. She held her head high, gazing imperiously at something beyond the picture frame. He looked at the left panel. A name had been carved into the wood in a swirling script, and below that, a date:

Gabriella della Signatura
A.D. 1445

He swallowed hard. This strange, beautiful object was more than five hundred years old, and he had taken it out of the museum. It was probably part of one of the displays. But why had it been in the worker's pocket? The question throbbed in his mind for a few seconds. It didn't matter, he told himself. He'd have to return it. But then his eyes returned to the woman in the painting, and he looked at her for a long time. He gently closed the panels and slipped the wooden locket into his desk drawer.

"Fall of the Roman Empire."

"400 A.D.," Eric replied automatically.

"Battle of Waterloo." His father hurled out the next question without a pause, shutting the front door behind him.

"1815."

"Discovery of the electric battery."

"Umm, 1800."

"By?"

"Alessandro Volta."

"Magna Carta signed when?"

"1200. No, wait. 1215."

"Good. Discovery of King Tut's tomb."

"1922."

"Name of the archaeologist."

"Howard Carter."

"Sinking of the Titanic."

"1912."

"Be more exact."

"April 12, 1912."

"Yes. First printing press."

Eric shook his head in defeat. "Don't know."

"Gutenberg press, 1440s. How could you forget the Gutenberg press? Without it, we wouldn't have any of these, not a single one." Mr. Sheppard waved his hand at the crammed bookcases as he crossed the living room. "In all, though, not bad."

It was a game they had always played, historical dates and facts, and his father would start it up without warning, while making dinner, walking down the street, reading a book.

"How was your day?"

"Well—"

But before Eric could go on, his father had sat down at the table and was hunched over the ancient typewriter, glaring at the piece of paper that curled out of it. He struck clumsily at the keys, cursed, and reached for the bottle of correction fluid. The fan was going full blast. Cans of tomato soup kept his tidy piles of handwritten notes from blowing away.

"There," he said after a few moments. "Had that sentence banging around in my head all the way home."

He shrugged off his conductor's jacket and let it fall to the floor beside the chair. His shirt was rumpled and damp. He yanked his tie loose.

Eric watched him staring intently at the typewriter, oblivious. Gone for the duration, Eric thought wryly, shaking his head. Eric had been waiting eagerly for his father to come home so he could tell him what had happened in the museum—waiting half the afternoon, damn it! But now it looked as if his latest story had him in the usual headlock.

Eric looked down at the book he'd been flipping through listlessly for the past hour. *Museums of the World*. He was only looking at the pictures. It was too hot to do anything else. His T-shirt was plastered against his back, and he was sure his dark hair was collecting the heat, storing it like solar coils. He pushed his hands through the thick curls and grimaced. He needed to get it cut.

He restlessly brushed away some bits of plaster that had flaked off the wall onto the cushions. The heat had been making it worse. It was an old house, long and narrow, with hardwood floors and crooked doorways and radiators that clanked noisily. It had been slowly falling apart for more than a hundred years. It was one of the last farm houses in the city, and certainly the only one downtown. It had been left to Eric's father years ago by *his* father—Eric's grandfather. Now it was sandwiched between two luxury highrise apartment buildings, and the side windows had been boarded up because they looked out onto concrete foundations.

"Damn!" his father said, reaching for the correction fluid again.

Eric thumbed through a few more pages of his book, unable to concentrate. Since he'd come back from the museum, he'd been trying to piece together the conversation he'd heard in the medieval gallery. But all that came back to him were unconnected phrases and sentences, puzzle pieces that didn't make any sense. He'd been thinking about the locket, too, or at least the woman in the painting. Why couldn't he get her face out of his mind? He glanced over at his father. Eric always felt guilty interrupting him when he was writing.

"I saw something really weird in the museum today," he finally blurted out.

"Tell me," his father said without looking up.

Eric waited for him to stop typing before he started. He told his father everything but stopped before the part about the locket. His father would want to see it, hold it, and Eric didn't want to share it with anyone.

"They were fighting right in the medieval armoury display?" his father asked.

"Yeah."

"That's a ridiculous place to fight," his father remarked. "They could have caused a lot more damage than they did. It's lucky they knocked over only the one soldier."

"No, Dad," Eric said, impatience creeping into his voice— he knew his father hadn't been listening very carefully. "The guy in black pushed it over on purpose. It happened before the fight."

"Was the armour all right?"

"Uh, yeah, I think so; I didn't—"

"What about the shield and sword?"

"They were fine, too, I think. It was only the soldier, the statue, that got busted up."

"They should really put up a glass shield. Those things are extremely old and valuable." He shook his head. "It's beyond me ... one of them actually picked up the shield?"

"The sword. I thought he was going to kill the other guy."

"Appalling. You don't just grab an antique sword that's centuries old and wave it around."

Eric traced the rip in his jeans. He couldn't tell his father that, in a strange way, he thought it was fitting the two men had fought in the middle of the display, surrounded by all those frozen soldiers holding weapons that hadn't been used for hundreds of years. His father would have been horrified.

His father was already looking back to the typewriter.

"Hey," Eric said. "Hello?"

"Hmm?"

"I mean, who do you think they were? Doesn't the whole thing sound weird to you?"

17

"I really—" His eyes were straying to the piles of paper on the table. "I really don't know, Eric. Look, I'm sorry; it's just that I'm at a really good part."

You're always just at a really good part, Eric thought. Lately, the stories seemed to be eating up more and more of his father's time. As soon as he got home from his shift on the subway, he'd start hacking away at the typewriter, sometimes not even stopping for dinner.

"You're going to love this one, Eric," his father said.

Probably, Eric thought grudgingly. He usually did. His father's stories were the strangest he'd ever read, but they were wonderful. The settings were cut off from the rest of the world, neither past nor present nor future. There were deserts and jungles and snow-capped mountains and angels with broken wings and magic cameras, and small towns overrun with cats, and sometimes, a woman with laughter like Nepalese wind chimes who disappeared down narrow streets into the twilight.

The woman, Eric felt certain, was his mother. She had died so soon after he was born that he had no memory of her. She had gotten caught in the subway doors, and the train hadn't stopped. His father had told him this when he was seven and he hadn't known how to react. Part of him wanted to laugh—it was impossibly horrible and absurd; the other part wanted to cry for the woman whose face he couldn't remember. But all he had done was watch his father's fingers as they traced a pattern on the tabletop, again and again.

His father never really talked about her, except in the stories, and Eric read them all hungrily, hoping to catch glimpses of his mother. He sometimes thought his father missed her as much now as when it had happened. There were periods when he seemed caught in a deep reverie—

18

days when he'd slip through the hours lifelessly, not writing, not talking much. There had been a few other women over the years, some of whom had even made breakfast in the mornings, but they never stayed longer than a month or two. And then his father would start a new story.

"Why haven't you ever tried to get them published?" Eric asked.

"I've never thought about it." He shrugged. "I do them for myself."

It made Eric angry to think of the pile of stories in his father's bedroom, yellowing with age.

"If you sold enough," he said, "maybe you wouldn't need to work on the subway anymore."

"It's as good a way to earn a living as any," his father said quietly. "It's certainly nothing to be ashamed of."

"That's not what I—"

"I've still made time for all this." He waved his hand to indicate the bookshelves. Self-taught. That was the word his father always used.

"That's not what I meant, anyway," Eric grumbled irritably, fanning out his shirt to cool his back. In fact, he wasn't sure quite what he'd meant. Maybe it *had* been intended as a small stab. But it couldn't be healthy, spending whole days in the subway tunnels, in the dark.

"I was thinking about you today," his father said distractedly.

Eric waited for him to go on.

"A book," he said, after hammering out a few more words on the typewriter. "A book that you should read."

"Oh," Eric said, disappointed.

"*Castle of Otranto* by Horace Walpole. I think you'd enjoy it."

Eric sighed. "Dad, you already gave that one to me. Remember? A couple of weeks ago."

19

"Oh. It's good, isn't it?"

"It was all right. It was kind of dumb."

"Kind of dumb?" His father looked up from his type-writer, scandalized. "It's a great classic."

Eric just nodded. Every old book was a great classic, according to his father. A shopping list would have been a great classic if it had been written a hundred years ago.

"You should try to read everything," his father said. "That's the only real education."

"You make it sound as if I picked up one book every five years," Eric said resentfully. "Chris thinks all I do is read."

"Well," his father said with a chuckle, "Chris isn't exactly an intellectual."

"You hardly know him!" Eric objected. "Last time he was over you didn't even say hello."

The lights flickered suddenly and the electric fan jolted in mid-revolution. The tiny television set in the corner switched on full blast.

Eric jumped. "Not again," he groaned.

"What a din," Mr. Sheppard said, gathering up his papers.

"It's been doing this all afternoon," said Eric. "Must be the heatwave."

"For most people," a dignified off-screen voice said, "shopping is not simply a pleasure, but a way of life. Here, in the heart of downtown, next door to the museum, a new shopping experience is about to be forged. More than four hundred new shops under one magnificent roof for the discriminating consumer. It's the mall of the future, for the way of the future, designed as a series of figure-eight patterns to encourage maximum shopper participation. Three kilometres of enclosed floor space, much of it totally underground, will take you effortlessly through an incomparable collection of the finest boutiques and eateries in the world. You'll be dazzled by neon, soothed by the sounds of our in-house music. It's all there for you, waiting. Elegance, simplicity, complicity. The new mall. Opening this fall."

"Complicity, for sure," growled Eric's father, shaking his head in disgust.

"Just another mall," Eric said with a shrug. "Chris told me this was one of his Mom's deals."

A news reporter appeared, standing across the street from a building that was spewing out smoke and flames. Eric recognized it as the rare-book library. He walked past it practically every day.

"The fire," the reporter shouted, "started early this morning at the corner of Main and Kierkegaard, and spread quickly out of control through the entire library. Firefighters have been working to stop the blaze, but many of the water hydrants in the immediate area have run dry. Filled with so much paper, this building is like a giant tinderbox. Just look at those books burn! This is the second fire in the downtown area within a week. Only three days ago, a well-known antiques dealership was the scene of a similar blaze, which destroyed most of the shop's merchandise and did millions of dollars of damage."

The reporter paused to watch as part of the library's wall collapsed outwards onto the street.

"At the scene," he said, turning to face the camera, "I'm Stuart Daw for Split Second News."

"Thanks, Stuart," said the studio anchor. "Just an incredible fire. And who needs it in this heat? Next, the latest in wrestling. Bob?"

"Well, Dirk, it was a good, good day for the Beast—"

It took Eric three tries to switch off the TV. When he

turned around, he was startled by the pallor of his father's face.

"It's a terrible thing," his father was saying. "One of the finest libraries in the world."

Eric watched his father.

"Floors and floors of books rising up all around you. They don't let you just browse, of course. You have to ask one of the librarians to get a particular book for you—and then you look at them under glass most of the time. But sometimes, you get to hold one. You can touch it, feel the old leather binding and the brittle pages, smell the old paper." A small smile fluttered across his mouth. "Once your mother—" He stopped suddenly and looked back down at the typewriter.

"What?" Eric said. He sat forward slightly.

But his father just shook his head. "Nothing."

Eric slumped back into the tattered upholstery of the sofa. It wasn't fair, he fumed inwardly. Why wouldn't he talk about her? Eric knew hardly anything about her; he'd never even seen a photograph. He suddenly thought of the locket, the tiny portrait inside.

"I wonder if they'll be able to save any of the books," his father muttered. "The worst thing is hardly anyone cares. Most people would rather watch the library burn on TV than read a book."

"Chris is probably watching it right now, eating popcorn," Eric said to annoy his father.

His father just nodded sadly.

"The whole city's been changing so fast, it's frightening," he said. "It's all so different from what it used to be."

"Lots of construction," Eric said.

"It's not just the construction," his father replied, waving his hand dismissively. "It's the whole city. It's getting too

22

big. It's getting too high. But it's also getting too forgetful. It can't even remember what it used to look like fifty years ago, twenty years ago, maybe even ten years ago. No wonder libraries burn. The city's eating itself up!"

Eric was used to his father's attacks on the city. His own thoughts were drifting back to the two men whispering in the medieval gallery. In a split second of total recall, he saw their dark shapes grappling, and the locket tumbling from Alexander's pocket. Gabriella della Signatura, he thought, what am I going to do with you?

3

Deep as the City

Chris scratched his short-cropped blond hair. "You know, when I first met you, I thought you were just another skinny geek—no offence, right?—but you do these crazy things. It's really more than five hundred years old?"

"I didn't know until I got home. I just pushed it right into my pocket. It could have been anything." Skinny geek. Great.

Chris shook his head in amazement. "You going to take it back?"

"I have to, don't I?" He had to force out the words. He'd spent a humid, restless night debating with himself. Returning it was the only right thing to do. But something about the locket—something about the woman's face—made him want to hide it away, to keep it for himself. He'd told Chris only because he was sure that, unlike his father, Chris wouldn't want to see it.

"You're not making this up, right?"

Eric shook his head and sighed. How many times did he have to go through this? "Chris, I saw it. They were fighting in the display, and the locket fell from the tall guy's pocket."

"You sometimes make things up, is why I'm asking. You tell me crazy things and I believe you and then I feel stupid."

"I haven't done that in a long time."

"Well, it's utterly weird. But I've heard weirder things lately. Did you watch the news this morning?"

"About the two guys who hijacked the window-washing platform and took it up to the thirtieth floor?"

"Uh-huh. It's the heat. It's making everyone utterly crazy."

They were strolling down Astrologer's Walk, a wide, tree-shaded lane that ran behind the museum. Eric looked up at the tall arched windows of clouded glass set into the blackened brick. On the other side of the path rose the gleaming shell of the new mall. It was nearly finished construction, a smooth veneer of steel and mirrored chrome supported by massive metallic buttresses and ventilation pipes. Work crews on scaffolding were fitting plates of glass onto the top level. The roar of winch motors and heavy machinery battered Eric's ears.

"Hey, that's a great rip," Chris said, nodding at Eric's jeans.

"My knee went through," Eric told him a little impatiently.

"Oh." Chris looked down at his own pair of designer jeans, which had a long slash above each knee and a second set of rips at mid-thigh. "Mine came this way. They make you pay for it, too, believe me. Costs a friggin' fortune."

"You buy them," Eric pointed out.

"Peer pressure," Chris countered. "Utterly beyond my control."

"Like the nose ring."

"You got it." He touched the metal stud in his nostril.

"What if driving a nail into your head comes into fashion?"

Skinny geek. That rankled him. Well, it was true enough. He glanced enviously over at Chris. He wasn't much taller than Eric, but he was a lot bigger, with broad shoulders and a filled-out chest. And Chris's jeans were solid-looking, the fabric falling in smooth, straight lines, unlike the baggy husks of his own pant legs. Chicken legs. Like father like son. He hated it. At least he didn't wear glasses. That would have been the final humiliation.

"So what did you want to show me?" he asked. Chris had called him early that morning, insisting that there was something he had to see at the new mall.

"Even you, techno-serf, will like this. It's utterly cool." He led Eric farther down the path and then pointed up at the steel wall of the shopping centre. "Take a look. They just installed it."

It was hard to miss, a huge cube of black glass the size of a house. Within its transparent walls swirled giant CD players and microwave ovens, refrigerators and televisions, watches and leather shoes, clothing with designer logos.

"Hologram billboard," Chris said. "And guess who suggested it?" He jabbed his thumb towards his chest. "I told Mom it would be great, and they actually did it! Utterly three-dimensional. Not bad, huh?"

"Very catchy," Eric said. Looking at it made him dizzy.

"You hate it, don't you?"

"No, I don't hate it!"

"You hate it; I can tell. You hate everything that runs off electricity. Techno-serf."

The glass-and-steel edifice seemed to quiver slightly and shift in the heat. A hot breeze stirred the sweat on Eric's forehead.

"I'm not a techno-serf."

"Right. You had trouble turning the school computer on."

"I'd never used one before," Eric protested.

"Utterly frightening."

"Why do you keep saying that word?" Eric exploded.

26

"'Utterly.' What is that, the adverb of the week?"

"Perhaps there's a better word you can teach me," said Chris, rolling his eyes.

"Yeah. 'Dictionary.' You are driving me *utterly* crazy!" He scrubbed the sweat out of his eyes with his fists.

"Pain in the ass," Chris muttered.

"No," Eric shot back. "What's a pain in the ass is being dragged out in thirty-five-degrees to look at some mall that looks like a building turned inside out!"

"If they added some Greek columns, would you be happy?" Chris said sarcastically.

"No. It'd still be ugly. It's a big metal cage. Why doesn't anyone think of anything original?"

"Designed by a world-famous architect, in case you're interested."

"How sad."

"Forget it, just forget it," Chris fumed. "Go back to the encyclopedia or whatever it is you're reading these days. All you ever do is read."

Eric looked away guiltily. Chris was right. In his spare periods at school, when most people went to smoke behind the gym or took off to the store, he sat in the library, going through the history books. His favourites were the ones with the illustrated time lines that charted important inventions and wars. Those were the best for memorizing dates. And there was something safe about dates. They didn't change. Easier to understand than people anyway—his father, his mother.

He glanced over at Chris, who still looked angry. Eric wasn't worried. They argued all the time. They enjoyed it in a way. They argued about anything: the quality of TV programming, a film they had just seen, the importance of computers, the importance of books, skyscrapers, noise

27

pollution, rock videos, sometimes the weather, and once, for almost an hour, about whose watch was more accurate, Eric's analog or Chris's digital.

Eric sometimes wondered why they were friends. At school, Chris was popular and usually hung around with the other guys on the soccer and basketball teams. Eric didn't know them. He might be a skinny geek, but they were all mentally impaired; they could barely write simple sentences. He'd rather stick it out alone. The only reason he had gotten to know Chris at all was that they were next-door neighbours—if you could call someone who lived fifty-six floors up a next-door neighbour. They took the subway to school together. Chris sometimes helped him with computer science. He sometimes helped Chris with history. That was about it. But this summer, they had been hanging out together a lot more, just because there was no one else around. It was convenient, and Chris was lazy when it came to anything other than sports. An elevator ride down to the ground floor was about all he could manage. So as the summer stretched on, Chris had been spending more time at their place, even though they had a tin-can television and no air-conditioning. He'd look around the house, like a dog sniffing out new territory. He'd look through the bookshelves, squint at the faded prints on the wall, settle into the dilapidated armchairs. And now, Eric was bothered when he thought that Chris's friendship might be just on loan for the summer. What would happen when school started up again? Goodbye, Chris? Probably.

"You think your father's really read all those books in your house?" Chris asked suddenly.

Eric nodded, grateful that the stand-off was over. "I think so."

"Pretty amazing."

"He reads most of them in his spare time while he's working on the subway. He never went to university or anything, so he's had to do it all himself. He just reads everything."

"Wow. Your dad's kind of weird. I mean, I like him and he seems like a nice guy, but he's just kind of weird."

Eric laughed awkwardly. He was used to people saying things like that about his father. But it still irked him, and made him feel as if he had to convince people that his father was perfectly normal. He was tired of defending him. Maybe they were right, after all—maybe his dad *was* weird.

"I've seen him a couple of times, writing on the subway," Chris said. "You can see all these sheets of paper in his little compartment. He must be really into it."

"He is," Eric said with a snort. "Believe me. He spends practically all his time writing lately."

Chris shook his head. "You know, I don't think he likes me very much."

"Sure he does." Eric knew he sounded fake.

"Nope. He thinks I'm utterly a moron. I can tell."

"He doesn't think you're a moron." It made Eric angry that his father hardly ever talked to Chris.

"He thinks I'm illiterate."

"Don't worry about it. He thinks I'm illiterate, too."

After a while Chris said, "You think he'll ever get married again?"

"Doubt it," Eric replied.

"Don't see why not, though. Some of my Mom's friends, they've been married four or five times, and they're not even that old, a lot of them." He laughed. "He could marry Mom!"

Chris's mother made a lot of money and was usually

away on business. She was a tall, forceful-looking woman with a deep, year-round tan. She said enthusiastic things like "Fantastic idea, a great thought, why don't we follow up on that?" and "It's a go-ahead from me." But she always looked rather preoccupied and restless when she was with Chris, as if she were still mentally working out the details of her latest real-estate project.

"Somehow, I don't think they'd work as a couple," Eric said with a grin, but he felt his smile contract fast. It would never work for his father, he thought, not with anyone. It wasn't normal, was it?

"How's *your* dad?" Eric asked, to change the subject.

"All right, I guess. He sent me this new software package from his shop. New graphics program. It's pretty good. Mom still hates it when he sends stuff to me. She doesn't say anything, but I can tell." He paused and then said, almost grudgingly, "Aw, Mom's okay, I guess."

Eric remembered Chris saying once that the only reason his father didn't get custody was that he sometimes hit the bottle a bit too hard—and Chris's mom made a lot more money. Eric knew that Chris would rather be living with his father. What would it be like to have two parents fighting over who got to keep you, fighting over who could love you better?

They'd nearly reached the end of Astrologer's Walk. Part of the path had been dug up by bulldozers and was strewn with blocks of concrete and metal girders. Eric paused at the edge of an open manhole and looked down.

"Deep as the city."

"What does that mean?" Chris wanted to know.

"Something my Dad always says. He says the city's as deep as it is high, but hardly anyone knows it."

"That's a long way down."

30

"He went down there once to explore, I think."

At the bottom of the concrete shaft, Eric could see several cylindrical tanks connected by rusted, pencil-thin pipes bristling with gauges and valves. Clamped to the wall of the tunnel were thicker, jointed pipes, and a metal duct that had been cut open, exposing a tangle of electrical cables.

"No," Chris said. "Forget it. No way."

"It wouldn't hurt to have a look." Eric pointed at the metal ladder that ran down the manhole. "It's not really that deep, anyway."

"Yeah, well, listen, I still haven't recovered from your last crazy little adventure."

"Oh, that."

"All because you were reading about the Roman baths or something."

"Ancient heating systems. I got a great mark on the project."

"All I remember is getting lost in the school steam tunnels and missing the next two periods."

"The furnace was deeper than I thought, that's all. But we found it."

"We got detentions."

"It was an educational opportunity not to be missed."

"It's too hot for this, Eric. Let's go back to my place. It's cool there. I'll show you the new graphics program."

"One very quick look. Come on, I looked at your hologram billboard."

"We'll play computer games. We'll shop on the Internet. We'll put tin foil in the microwave and make lightning. You got off on that last time."

"That *was* kind of fun. We'll do that after."

"I'm claustrophobic."

"You are *not* claustrophobic. You know, for a superjock, you're not very adventurous. C'mon, you can flex your biceps on the way down the ladder. Aren't you even curious?"

"Well, no. It's just the stuff that makes the city work. No big deal. Pipes and wires and cables and drains. Stuff like that, right?"

"I've always wanted to see. You coming?" He lowered himself down the ladder. A faint hiss, like the sound of someone wheezing, filled the tunnel. Wisps of steam curled out from the valves of one of the cylindrical tanks. The stale air, close with heat and moisture, had a pungent edge to it.

"What's the smell?" Chris asked, stepping down beside him.

"Oh, ye of the electric oven," Eric chided him. "It's just gas. Our stove at home smells the same when the element doesn't light right away." He tapped against one of the pipes with his knuckles. "From these, I guess."

"Is it safe?"

"Completely nontoxic."

Chris stood with his hands in his pockets, nodding his head in mock appreciation. "Okay," he said. "Well, this has been great, Eric, a real treat. Thank you."

"Hang on," Eric said. He looked along the rectangular tunnel. It stretched out in two directions, lit by electric lamps hooked onto the wall. "I just want to see how far it goes."

"What do you mean, how far it goes? It probably goes halfway out to the suburbs!"

"Come on, I promise you'll be back in time for the sitcoms."

"I don't know why I let you drag me into this crap. There're probably construction workers down here. We're going to get into trouble. This is utterly stupid."

32

Eric wasn't listening. He was too busy taking everything in. Bundles of frayed electrical cables hung from the ceiling like jungle vines; condensation dripped from the rust-stained couplings of sagging pipes; the needles of large round meters clicked noisily from side to side, as if monitoring a huge heartbeat.

The tunnel suddenly opened out onto a metal platform, like one of those old-fashioned fire escapes on the outsides of buildings. Eric squinted into the pitch darkness. He couldn't see a thing. But suddenly, a feeling of vertigo hit him in the pit of his stomach. He looked down at the darkness seeping through the metal chinks in the grilled floor.

They were standing over an immense chasm. From somewhere in the distance came the muffled roar of a passing subway train. A hot breeze moved against Eric's face.

"I think Dad was right, " he said to Chris, and his words seemed to dissolve in the air the moment they left his mouth. He moved cautiously to the railing and peered down.

"Can you see anything?" Chris asked.

"No, but it feels as if it goes on forever."

"All I can see are different shades of black," Chris remarked.

A drawn-out mechanical groan drifted up to them from the darkness.

"Is that the subway again?" Chris said.

"I don't—"

Hundreds of metres below, they saw a small, but intense spark of light. And the sound rose again. No, it couldn't be the subway. Eric knew that sound perfectly, the clattering rush getting louder, then fading away as the train passed by. This was a slow, heavy clanking that filled the air with a hum, like the throbbing of insects. Eric felt it through his teeth and stomach, through the metal platform beneath his feet.

Another spark. The hum deepened. Eric felt the first bat-wing stirrings of panic moving through his body. He watched his hands on the metal railing trembling with the vibration. A rivulet of sweat slithered jaggedly down his cheek. There was something terrifying about that noise. What was it coming from?

For a split second, his nose tingled with the sting of sulphur, and then, without any warning, a billowing cloud of dense, dark smoke boiled up from the blackness and washed over them. Eric recoiled, coughing, his face and eyes burning with soot.

"What's down there?" Chris gasped, covering his face with his hands.

They stumbled back towards the tunnel. The only thought circling through Eric's mind, like some nursery-school refrain, was that the city was burning, burning, burning, the city was burning.

4

Breakdown on the Line

Tomorrow would be soon enough. He'd take it back tomorrow.

Eric held the locket closer to his desk lamp. He'd been studying the woman's portrait for the past hour. He could guess from her name that she was Italian, and the date was clear, but he wanted to know more—how old she was, how she lived back then, what her family was like, whether she was kind or cruel, how that incredible mane of hair smelled, warmed by the sunlight. And he wanted to know whom or what she was glaring at beyond the picture frame. What made her eyes shine like that?

His thumb had left a small smudge on the edge of the panel. He carefully brushed it away and then looked at his hands. Even after taking a shower, he still had soot on his fingertips. He hadn't seen Chris so angry since the furnace adventure. When they had climbed out of the manhole, Chris's blond hair had been darkened by the thick cloud of smoke, his face streaked with grime. He had vowed right there never to listen to any more of Eric's crazy skinny-geek ideas again. But Eric wasn't worried: he'd heard it all before. Chris always came around.

An advertising blimp droning past overhead made the house vibrate. Eric's eyes were drawn back to the locket. She was beautiful. He didn't want to give it back. But he knew he had to. He could always leave it where Alexander had dropped it in the armoury. No. If he did that, he'd never find out anything about her. He'd find Alexander, call him up at the museum. He could just say he'd happened across the locket while going through the armoury—he wouldn't even have to mention the fight or the man in black. Eric juggled the idea around in his head for a few minutes. All he'd say was that he'd found it lying there. He'd seen the worker in the display earlier, taking away a sword and shield, and assumed it was his. The story wasn't watertight, but it would probably give him the chance to ask some questions.

He pushed his chair back and stretched his arms over his head with a groan. His eyes roved restlessly over the paper models on his dresser top—the Roman baths, the Parthenon, the Globe Theatre—and then settled on a small collection of lead soldiers that his father had given him years ago. Some were crouched low, taking aim with their old-fashioned rifles; others were running, sabres raised.

Why don't you just give it to me?

The sentence slithered through his mind without warning. Eric could suddenly see the man in black, pushing against the life-sized medieval soldier, a sneer twisting the corner of his mouth. He felt the pressure of gravel against his hands, the ache in his bent knees. His nostrils wrinkled with the smell of oil and machinery. Then it was over, like a short loop of film played through a projector.

Eric shook his head. It was too weird. He dragged a piece of paper from his desk drawer, made two columns, one for Alexander and one for the guy in black, and started listing everything he knew. The guy in black was after something, but what? He was young, and he'd changed his name—Eric remembered that now: he'd said he had a brand new one. And he was obviously a jerk because he'd wrecked the soldier statue. That was about it. As for Alexander, it was pretty clear he worked at the museum. He was old, had a strange-sounding voice and a bad cough, and could speak in a foreign language. And he carried a five-hundred-year-old locket around with him. But how strange was that, really? Maybe he was just taking it to be cleaned.

He read over the list a couple of times and then crumpled it up with a derisive snort. He hardly knew a thing. Certainly nothing that was going to tell him what they were fighting over. Whatever it was, he thought, it had to be pretty important.

He hauled himself out of his chair and went downstairs to get a drink. The television had switched itself on again, and he watched as a wrecking ball swung into the side of an old building down by the docks. The building's stone face crumpled away. Bits of tall columns tumbled to the ground in a swirl of rubble and dust. Eric could make out half of a broken arch in the ruin. A Split Second News reporter appeared and began talking about the new office complex that would fill the space. Dad was going to have a fit.

Eric turned the TV off. It immediately turned itself back on. Eric unplugged it and walked to the window. The roads sweated tar. Buildings seemed to tremble on their foundations. On the museum steps, a man in underpants stood beside a small portable refrigerator, loudly auctioning off packets of ice cubes.

Time for another cold shower.

His father's face was pale and drawn. "Breakdown on the line this afternoon," he said almost apologetically, as if wanting to explain away his haggard appearance.

"What happened?" Eric asked him.

Mr. Sheppard shrugged. "No one knows exactly. The

electricity got cut off somehow, just before the museum station. There was a shower of blue sparks, and the train slid to a dead stop."

"For how long?"

"Two hours or so."

"Get any writing done?"

"We were in total darkness the whole time." He was looking past Eric, through the walls, out across the city. "What did you do today?"

"Nothing."

There was no point. Eric had seen his father wrapped up in himself like this lots of times. And he'd seen this one coming. Yesterday, after that news spot on the fire at the rare-book library and all through dinner, he'd barely said a word. Then he had gone back to his typewriter but had only written a sentence or two. And in the middle of the night, Eric had been woken by the creaking of floorboards—the sound of pacing. He could see light coming under his father's door from the hallway. For a few terrifying moments, he had thought he could hear quiet crying, but it had turned out to be a vagrant cat prowling the hot night streets.

"Nothing at all," Eric said again, anger stealing into his voice. He wasn't even going to try to tell his father about the open manhole or about how deep the city was, and what was down there. Dad would just sit there, nodding mechanically, lost in his own thoughts.

Eric heaved himself out of the armchair and headed towards the stairs. He felt as if he were suffocating in the living room. He was sick of it. Always thinking of her. Or writing about her. She was dead, had been for thirteen years! If his father only thought about him as much as he did her—*half* as much, a *fraction* as much! Dad wouldn't even talk about her.

38

"The *Mona Lisa*!" his father called out before he'd reached the stairs.

"Leonardo da Vinci."

"Painted in what year?"

"1503."

"Eruption of Mount Vesuvius."

"79 A.D."

"Good. War of the Roses."

"1450."

"Between what two families?" There was hardly any enthusiasm in his voice.

"York and Lancaster."

"Right. Columbus's discovery of America."

"Dad—"

"You know this one!"

"Why do you hide the pictures of her?" He thought of the wooden locket upstairs in his drawer, wrapped up in an old washcloth.

"What?" His father looked shaken.

"Photos of her—" He searched for a better word; they talked about her so rarely. "*Her.*"

"Well," his father began hesitantly, but then trailed off, like a voice at the end of a long-distance phone line, dissolving in static.

"Why haven't you ever shown me?" Eric pressed on, insistent. "There are pictures." He remembered once, several years ago, he'd walked into his father's room to find him slowly turning the pages of a large book. Looking up, startled, his father had quickly closed it, and Eric had automatically thought he had done something wrong. But even then, instinctively, he had thought, *It was her*. He had never seen the thick volume again, and his father had never mentioned it.

"Why are you asking that all of a sudden?"

All of a sudden. That was a laugh. All Eric had to do was look at his father and see that spark of sadness in his eyes to know he was thinking about her. So why did he get to keep her all to himself? Eric had only the woman in the stories: elusive, fiercely loving, fiercely indifferent, very stubborn, very strong. He immediately thought again of the portrait of Gabriella della Signatura.

"I'm curious about her," he told his father. "That's normal, isn't it?"

"Of course," his father said. "Perfectly normal."

There was a bitterness in his voice that Eric hadn't heard before. Suddenly it was as if he didn't know the tall, bony man sitting rigidly on the sofa, his fingers pulling gently at the tweed upholstery. Eric stood in the doorway, afraid to say anything.

"There are some pictures," his father said, with a forced-looking smile. "But not now, all right? I don't know where they are, and I'm very tired. I'll show them to you later, okay?"

"Sure."

He looked away from his father's tired face and headed upstairs.

"I don't know his last name," Eric said into the phone.

There was a pause at the other end of the line. "No," said the museum switchboard operator. "We don't have anyone here with that name, first or last."

"Are you sure?" Eric asked. "Alexander. I'm sure he works there."

"I'm sorry." The voice sounded impatient now. "It's not on my list. There is no one here by that name."

The shadows of twilight were just beginning to stretch across the city when Eric stepped out onto the street. The heat wrapped itself around him like a damp wool cloak. But he needed to get out, get away from his father's brooding silence and fake smiles.

Across the road, the museum shone in the bright wash of its floodlights. Why wasn't Alexander on the switchboard list? Eric hadn't gotten the name wrong; he was sure of that. The man in black had definitely called the silver-haired man Alexander. And Alexander obviously worked there: the coveralls, the careful way he had picked up the toppled sword and shield, his final disappearance through a hidden door at the back of the display. So why wasn't he listed in the directory?

Eric crossed the street and turned down Astrologer's Walk. Up ahead, he could see green light from the hologram billboard sweeping across the walk and the museum wall.

If he couldn't call Alexander, the best he could do was go back to the museum in the morning and wait around in the hopes of seeing him again. Or he could try to find that door. It probably led to the back of the museum, to the storerooms and workshops. He looked up at the high arched windows that faced onto Astrologer's Walk. Back there, behind the clouded glass.

"Clank, clank, clank yourself!"

Eric started in surprise and looked into the shadows against the museum wall. A man in tattered clothing stood holding a fishing rod, yelling down into a storm drain grate. Eric had seen him before, lots of times. Jonah—that was the name Eric and his father had given him. He was always surrounded by garbage bags bulging with newspaper, and talking to himself. In the summer he fished through the storm drain grates behind the museum, lowering his line deep into the city and, if what Eric had heard from his father was true, occasionally reeling in a catch. Eric had never seen him so agitated.

"Dry as a whale's skeleton in a desert!" Jonah blustered, throwing his fishing rod to the ground. He wiped the back of his hand across his mouth. "Fire and brimstone. You! Come here."

Jonah was talking directly to Eric now, motioning to him urgently. He held back. Jonah was crazy, like all the other people who lived on the streets, shouting on corners, huddling in alcoves. But he looked harmless enough. And he was waving so insistently that Eric found himself stepping slowly closer.

He stopped a few feet away. He'd never been close enough to see how worn down Jonah was. His face was stubbled and sun-cured like leather. He seemed to be wearing fragments of several different shirts, wrinkled and layered with dirt, and a baggy pair of grey trousers with pockets all up and down the legs. He gave off a strong smell, too: sweat and mildew and something chemical. Like rug cleaner, Eric thought, and his nostrils contracted involuntarily in revulsion.

"No more," Jonah was muttering urgently, ducking his head. "Gone, all of them. No more water." He stabbed his finger down at the cast-iron grate.

"You haven't caught any fish lately?" Eric asked, glancing at the fishing rod and tangle of line.

Then Jonah looked him straight in the face, and Eric saw his eyes for the first time. They were startlingly clear, gleaming brightly in his crumpled face.

"Fire and brimstone!" Jonah shouted, and before Eric had time to step back or raise his arm, Jonah had lunged forward and seized his bony shoulders.

"Hey," Eric began. "What—?" He tried to wrench himself free, but Jonah's grip was too strong; his fingers levered into Eric's skin like claws.

"Down, underneath, down there, down," Jonah yelled, spittle collecting at the corners of his mouth. "Smoke and hot air, clank, clank, clank. Fire and brimstone."

"Right, yeah," Eric said. The few people on the path hurried by with their heads turned in the other direction. Great, that was just great; he could be getting a knife put through him and everyone would just pretend they didn't see anything. What a city.

"No, listen," Jonah said, and his voice was now softer and slower. His eyes were clear and deep. "Fire and brimstone. You tell them inside—" He nodded up at the museum wall. "Tell them, yes?"

"All right," Eric stammered, nodding. "All right; yes." He'd promise anything if Jonah would just let go.

Jonah released his grip and turned to his plastic garbage bags. "Away all the fish, no more," he mumbled to himself as if Eric weren't there, had never been there.

Eric looked back over his shoulder as he walked away. Crazy idiot. Except that ...

Clank, clank, clank. That was the noise he and Chris had heard from the underground platform. So Jonah had heard it, too. But the rest was just junk—sounded like the guy who stood on the street corner preaching about the wrath of God. Just crazy words that didn't make any sense.

43

"Fire and brimstone," he muttered. The words rang through his head.

5

Alexander

Someone was watching him.

Eric paused in the entrance hallway of the museum and looked around. Just a few other visitors, the usual knot of people heading for the gift shop. Nerves, he told himself. There was no one watching him. He shivered in the air-conditioned cool. It was either too hot or too cold. There was no in-between these days.

But it happened again. As he climbed the swirling stairs, he could feel eyes boring into the top of his skull, and when he looked quickly up, he was sure he saw someone moving back from the railing on the level above him. And a few minutes later, as he walked through the Chinese tomb, he thought he saw something shift at the back of the display.

Stop, he told himself. You're freaking yourself out.

He did a quick tour of the museum, watching for Alexander, and by the time he reached the medieval gallery, his hands were numb with cold, and a muscle in his thin chest was stuttering like a telegraph signal. He pushed his right hand into his pocket and wrapped his fingers gently around the locket, feeling its bevelled corners through the wash-cloth.

A few visitors passed through the armoury, including one man who panned a video camera rapidly from side to side as he strolled down the corridor without stopping.

Eric walked slowly through the darkened gallery. The stillness of the displays unnerved him, the soldiers and horses frozen in mid-action, as if they might suddenly jolt to life and finally finish swinging their swords, raising their shields, spurring their horses. A hundred pairs of eyes. The skin on his forearms crawled.

There was no sign of Alexander. What are my chances of finding him like this anyway, Eric wondered. Very slight. He tried to rub away the goose bumps on his right arm. He grimaced, wishing he could get some meat on his bones. He leaned against the railing and gazed into the display. The toppled soldier had been removed, leaving only the imprint of boots on the gravel. Eric looked deeper back, into the shadows.

The door blended in so well with the painted backdrop that he never would have noticed it if it hadn't been left slightly ajar. A vertical sliver of light from the opening gave it away. He looked at it for a long time, chewing thoughtfully on his lower lip. His fingers drummed softly against the locket.

He walked to the far end of the gallery to give himself time to think. It wouldn't hurt to have a look. His chances of finding Alexander back there would be better than if he were to wait in the galleries all day. And if he got caught he could always plead ignorance. He turned and started back.

He was alone. He swung his legs over the railing and scuttled through the petrified army. The soldiers followed him with their dead eyes. He reached the sliver of light in the dark wall, wedged his fingers into the gap and pulled the door open just far enough for his slim body to slip through.

A long corridor, illuminated by fluorescent lights, stretched out ahead of him. His heart and breathing slowed. Turning around to face the huge door, he saw that it was marked: West Armoury. He must be in one of the service corridors that ran behind the displays and into the back of the museum.

He started walking, going over what he would say to Alexander. Found the locket. Saw you disappearing through the door. Assumed it was yours. Came to give it back. Fine. And then he'd try to work in some questions about the locket, and about Gabriella della Signatura.

The passageway branched in three directions, and Eric picked one at random. He could hear the distant sounds of voices, and the low rumble of wheels under a heavy load. But it was impossible to tell where they were coming from. He passed more and more junctions, other corridors and stairs, some going up, others down. Rat's maze, he thought.

It suddenly occurred to him how absurd all this was. Did he really expect to find Alexander back here? He could wander for hours, and then probably just get caught by some other worker. Just to find out about some woman in an old locket. Crazy. Alexander probably didn't know anything about her anyway.

He was about to turn back when the sound of footsteps sent an icy contraction through his stomach. He had reached a large intersection of passages and stairs. He paused, holding his breath so he could listen better. The footsteps seemed to be coming from behind him, then up ahead, then to his left ... getting louder.

Well, he thought, his mouth suddenly dry, this is it.

"'I saw Eternity the other night / Like a great ring of pure and endless light, / All calm, as it was bright ...'"

The words seemed to well up from the air around Eric, from the tiled floor, the brick walls.

"'Our life is short, and our days run / As fast away as does the sun ...'"

Eric heard a cough, and at that moment, Alexander came

47

into view around the corner, once again dressed in blue coveralls, a tool satchel slung over his shoulder and bouncing against his hip. He stopped when he saw Eric, but only the mildest look of surprise crossed his face. His eyes flashed over Eric intently, as if studying every feature.

"Have you lost your way?" Alexander asked in his peculiar, hoarse voice.

About sixty or so, Eric guessed. And he hadn't noticed the first time how thin Alexander was, the straps of his coveralls stretched over razor-edged shoulders, his pant legs baggy. His hands were long and slender, his fingers almost skeletal, his wrists pinched and knobby. The veins of his narrow forearms stood out prominently against his skin, like elastic cord binding him tightly together. He's skinnier than me, Eric thought gratefully.

He tried to moisten his parched mouth.

"I—" he began, but faltered. He could feel the tiny weight of the locket in his pants pocket. And he suddenly realized that he didn't want to give it back. He couldn't bring himself to draw it out of his pocket and surrender it to this stranger.

"Yeah, I kind of got lost," he said quickly.

"I see," said Alexander, his eyes still locked on Eric's.

There was something about the twist of Alexander's mouth and his intonation that made Eric think Alexander knew he was lying. Sweat prickled at the back of his neck. Was it possible Alexander knew about the locket? There was no way he could. Still, the look in the man's eyes made Eric feel that he was being peeled like an onion, layer by layer.

"That's exceedingly unfortunate," Alexander was saying. There it was again, Eric thought, that slight edge of mocking disbelief in his voice. "Shall I escort you back to the galleries, then?" He gestured to one of the passages.

"Thanks," Eric said. Neither moved, as if they both knew the truth of the matter, but were choosing to play this game.

"Your face is a familiar one," Alexander said. "I'm certain I've seen you before."

"I come here a lot," Eric responded, a spark of uneasiness flickering in his mind, the feeling he'd had earlier of being watched. "Especially since it's been so hot."

"Ah, yes, that's right," Alexander said, as if he'd only been vaguely aware of the heatwave outside. "And of course, that is why I remember you. But I've seen you here on numerous occasions, even earlier. With your father I believe."

"Yeah, well, we live just across the road."

"In one of those glittering towers of Babel?"

Eric was puzzled for a moment. "Oh," he said with a nervous chuckle. "You mean the highrises. No, we live in the old house—" And then he stopped. He couldn't believe he was telling these things to a complete stranger.

"The old farm house between the two towers," Alexander said pleasantly.

"Yeah, that's the one." Eric tried without success to hold back a shiver. But then again, he told himself, there was only one old house across the road—theirs.

"I am continually surprised at its longevity in this city," Alexander commented. "It is an extremely rare find."

"Dad won't sell it." He was doing it again, just letting things slip out.

"Oh? Why is that?" Alexander's creased face showed interest, but Eric thought there was something insincere-sounding about the question, as if the man already knew the answer.

"He likes old things," Eric said curtly. But it was more because of Mom, he thought. Because he lived there with her and now he can't bring himself to sell it.

"Ah," Alexander said. "And you must take after your father."

"What do you mean?" Eric asked sharply. Comparisons with his father always made him uncomfortable—and coming from a stranger, they made him wary, too.

"The simple fact that you spend so much time here would seem to indicate that you like old things as well."

"Oh. Yeah." Eric looked away. Alexander's eyes seemed to tear through him. He knew about the locket. Why didn't he say anything? Eric forced himself to calm down. Alexander couldn't know anything about the locket. He was making himself paranoid over nothing. Just cool it.

"Visitors are not usually permitted past the galleries," Alexander was saying. "But if you would like, I could show you through the workshops. I only offer because I think you might find them interesting."

Eric looked up at him. "I'd like that," he said carefully.

"Very well. These are the service corridors," Alexander explained, indicating the passages that led off from the junction. "They twine like serpents through the back of the museum, behind most of the displays. Why don't we go this way?"

He fell into a long-striding gait. Walking quickly beside him, Eric was aware of his strong odour; not unpleasant exactly, it was the same musty smell his father's sweaters had when they were first taken out of the trunk at the beginning of winter—a thick smell of wool and mothballs.

"Are you a repairman here?" Eric asked.

Alexander nodded. "I tend to the exhibits, perform minor repairs and so on. Now, the central workshops are what you would find most engaging, I think. Am I walking too quickly for you? I hardly think so. You're keeping up nicely. One should always make the most of one's time. 'But at my back I always hear / Time's wingèd chariot hurrying near ...' You know the rest, of course."

The strange thing was that he did. It must have been his father—something his father used to read. The next two lines rose to the surface of his mind.

"'And yonder all before us lie / Deserts of vast eternity,'" he found himself saying.

"That's it!" exclaimed Alexander. "Marvellous stuff." His voice had clouded over and he coughed violently for a few seconds. "Excuse me," he said, choking out the words. "A small pestilence—a cold, rather."

Eric glanced up. Such an old-fashioned way of talking. Would a repairman really talk like that, and recite old poetry, too? Snobbery, he chided himself. His father the subway conductor would not approve.

Eric watched Alexander walking slightly ahead of him, jackknife legs, thin arms lost in the folds of his coverall sleeves. Eric thought of the fight in the armoury, and couldn't believe Alexander had been able to hold his own against the man in black. He should have been snapped like a dry twig. Still, there was a kind of strength to the man, as if he'd been whittled down to the hard, bare essentials.

They'd come to a dead end. Alexander went up to the wall and, with a flourish of his hand, pressed a button.

"Freight elevator," Eric said, and Alexander turned and winked.

A deep groan rose from the depths of the shaft and swiftly grew louder. There was a jarring thud, a brief silence, and then the whole wall seemed to split horizontally as the massive doors opened.

Alexander pushed aside the metal gate and ushered Eric inside. The elevator was almost as large as Eric's room at home. Alexander pressed a button and the elevator gave a mighty lurch. Eric could see the rough stone walls of the shaft slide by. He counted four floors before they came to a shuddering halt.

Stretched out before him was a colossal workshop, throbbing with machinery. Light slanted in broad beams through the high, arched windows—the same ones, Eric realized, that faced onto Astrologer's Walk. Thousands of specks of dust danced and glowed in the air.

Two workers brushed past Eric, carrying wooden planks. Ahead, he saw a line of men pushing wheelbarrows full of stone blocks across the crowded floor. Another group carried huge plates of glass, balanced precariously against their shoulders. Workers were hunched intently over machines, shouting out orders. A tide of noise washed over him: the pounding of hammers, the sharp serrated sound of saws, the growl of motors powering huge drills, the sudden snap of arc welders. His nostrils twitched with the scent of dust and wood, oil and heated metal.

"It's a glorious sight, isn't it?" Alexander said with a continental sweep of his arm. "Does it not make your heart quicken? This is the machine works. Orders are delivered here from every department in the museum—glass for display cases, chicken-wire for a papier-mâché backdrop, hinges for doors, steel to reinforce a dinosaur's tail, timber to replace a broken plank on the Spanish galleon. An endless stream of requests! This way."

Eric followed Alexander across the vast room, past the rows of throbbing machinery, benches and tables, towards a spiral staircase that corkscrewed up against the far wall. They climbed the clanging steel steps to a high catwalk.

Eric gazed out over the workshop. He could see it all now, a shifting collage of machine parts and bodies, metal levers and arms, wheels and human heads, all moving in rhythmic unison. He felt drunk with the swirling noise and activity below.

But suddenly the huge ceiling lamps flickered, the machinery stuttered. Eric stiffened. Again, and this time the lights went out completely, and the roar of the machines gradually faded to a quiet whirring, then silence.

Eric quickly looked over. Alexander was standing very tall and still, watching the workroom. He didn't seem even to be breathing. Only a few seconds passed before the lights blinked on again and the machinery kicked in, sounding like airplane turbines warming up.

"Happens at our house all the time," Eric said. "It's the heatwave."

"Yes," said Alexander after a few moments. He looked back at Eric. "Now then, shall we continue? The department workshops continue on either side of us, and above us, as well. That's where the real creation takes place."

"I'd like to see them all," Eric said.

"Yes. I knew you would!" Alexander exclaimed. "Mesopotamian, Egyptian, Greek and Roman, West Asian, European, Oriental, American, African, Paleontology, Ornithology, Earth Sciences ..." His list was cut short by another coughing fit, more violent than the first. "The dust!" he proclaimed. "The dust is the cause. It is of no consequence. This way. Let me show you."

Eric felt another quick stab of suspicion. It was almost as if Alexander had expected him. Was it chance that they had met in those tunnels? When you thought about how big the building was .... And Alexander seemed to know quite a lot about him. He hadn't even asked Eric his name—hadn't offered his own either, as if he assumed Eric already knew. Which Eric in fact did.

He followed Alexander along the catwalk and through a doorway into the next room, as large as the first. Below, surrounded by a network of scaffolding, a dinosaur was under construction. Workers clung to the metal latticework like spiders, painting the creature's head, welding together pieces of its long tail in little bursts of light and smoke. A woman was varnishing the dinosaur's toenails. The room was cluttered with workbenches, their surfaces hidden under reference books, blueprints and tools. Tall shelves and cupboards lined the walls, filled with giant dinosaur bones.

Eric felt a wave of nostalgia—all those visits to the dinosaur gallery together—and now he and his father couldn't even talk. Dad would be too preoccupied, not paying attention.

"You have fond memories of the dinosaur gallery, no doubt," Alexander said.

"It used to be one of our favourite parts, me and my father," Eric told him.

"And now?"

"We don't come together as much anymore. He's been pretty busy lately."

He knew he shouldn't be talking like this, but it seemed so easy. The tall, stooped man was watching him closely, nodding.

"Is he a very busy man, your father?"

"He's a subway conductor, and he writes a lot in his spare time."

Alexander nodded again. "Shall we go on? There are several other workshops you'll find of interest."

He led Eric to the window of a workroom where a

scholar poured over a misshapen tablet of stone, its surface covered in hieroglyphics. Through another window Eric saw a team of men and women polishing a suit of armour. Further on, a man sat in a small library, books spread out all around him, his head bowed in concentration.

"I once worked in a library," Alexander was saying into his ear. "A vast library, with the finest collection of literature in the world. We had some half a million volumes, which was a breathtaking number in those days."

"Here in the city?" Eric asked.

"Oh no, not here—and it's gone now. It burned down many years ago. Everything was lost. It was a great tragedy. Those were things that will never be recovered."

Eric glanced at Alexander. It was uncanny how much he had sounded like Dad.

"And there have recently been fires here as well, did you know?" Alexander went on in a conversational tone. "One at the rare-book library, another at the antiquarian's. Perhaps you've seen the news reports. People have always craved a good fire."

"My father says that people would rather watch the fires on TV than read a book."

"Or go to the museum. People place little value on such things now."

Like the man in black, Eric almost said. The man who had knocked over the soldier. Who was that guy? he wondered. But he knew he couldn't ask, not without giving away the fact that he'd been hiding in the display during the fight.

"Shall we continue?" Alexander said.

They passed like ghosts through the tangle of corridors. Mounting a twisting set of stairs, they came to another room, where Oriental carpets and tapestries were being sprayed for bugs. At the next workshop, his face pressed close against the window, Eric looked on as shards of pottery were glued back together to form ancient vases.

He devoured everything. He felt as if history were being resurrected before his eyes.

"There is a great deal more to show you," Alexander said, "but I haven't much more time."

"What's below us, on the lower floors?" The buttons on the freight elevator had continued much farther down than the one Alexander had pressed.

"Those are the storage rooms, the treasure houses of Kubla Khan! There is space in the galleries, you see, to display only a minuscule portion of the museum's collection, so the remainder is packed carefully away."

"How far down do they go?"

"To the very pit of hell!" Alexander proclaimed with a dramatic flourish. "Ah, forgive me. A jest—a joke, rather. Let me see ... twenty floors, I believe." He looked thoughtful for a moment. "No, perhaps only eighteen. The two lowest levels have been barricaded for many years now. They sealed them up during the renovations because there was a problem with water leakage from the storm drains."

Deep as the city, Eric thought, and the clanging of machinery in the darkness rang through his head.

"Is there anything down there still?" he asked. He could still see Jonah bent over the storm drain grate, bellowing about fire and brimstone.

"Not a thing," Alexander replied. "They are empty as tombs, home only to rats." He tried to stifle a cough but couldn't.

"Are you all right?" Eric looked at him with concern. "Isn't there something you could take for that?"

"A passing fit." His breathing calmed and his eyes settled

on Eric. "How much did you see and hear in the armoury?"

Eric's body tightened and, for a moment, he felt sick. He had been watched without his knowing. Even though he'd hidden in the shadows of the display, Alexander had known he was there.

"Alexander's not your real name," he shot back to cover up his alarm. "I called the museum."

"I see." The tall, stooped man appeared amused, a small spark dancing in each pupil. "I applaud your resourcefulness. But it is my real name—my middle name, in fact. It is simply that no one calls me by it."

"Only the man you fought with?"

"Yes. Your ears are very sharp. You heard everything, *saw* everything?" His gaze was piercing.

Eric couldn't stand it any longer.

"Here," he said, reaching into his pocket. "I found it on the floor afterwards." He unfolded the washcloth and held out the locket. "You dropped it, right? That's why I came. To give it back."

Alexander's bony hand darted out and closed around the wooden oblong.

"I've been searching for this," he said.

A chill ran through Eric. His instincts told him that Alexander was lying: he'd known all along where it was. Alexander had dropped it on purpose, left it like a lure. Everything seemed to click into place: the feeling of being watched, the door at the rear of the display left slightly ajar, the meeting in the service corridor. Had it really all been planned out, every step? But why?

For a split second he wanted to get as far away as possible. But he stood riveted, watching the rapt expression on Alexander's face as he gazed at the locket.

"There she is," he said softly. "A wonderful likeness,

though it fails to capture her fully—or so I am told. But even Leonardo fell short with his *Mona Lisa*. Yes, truly one of the great beauties. 'Love, that doth reign and live within my thought, / And built his seat within my captive breast.' "

The smile faded from Alexander's lips, and he looked up at Eric.

"Why didn't you give it back immediately?" he demanded.

There was no anger in his voice, only a fierce urgency.

"Well—" Eric faltered. "I—"

"Tell me!"

"I wanted to keep it," Eric heard himself saying. "I didn't want to give it back."

"Yes, yes," Alexander said softly, urging him on. "And why?"

"Because it was old and beautiful." He scarcely recognized his own voice. "Because of her. There was something about her." How could he explain the mesmerizing effect she had? "I wanted to know about her, more than just her name and date. I wanted it, her, for myself—to keep her safe. I didn't want anyone else to have it."

"That's right, yes," said Alexander quietly, his eyes ablaze. How strange they were, Eric noticed for the first time: a swirling ocean green, infinitely deep.

The lights went out with an electric snap, plunging the corridor into darkness. A second later came a ghostly fluorescent flicker that lasted long enough for Eric to make out the stricken look on Alexander's face. Then blackness again.

"'The day is done, and the darkness / Falls from the wings of Night, ...' " Alexander's voice was a hoarse, croaking whisper in the dark. For the first time Eric felt afraid.

The lights flared on. Alexander's face was tight and pale.

58

A muscle twitched at the corner of his mouth. His fingers tightened around the locket.

"This heatwave," Eric said, watching Alexander nervously. "It's really messing up the city."

"No. It's not the heatwave."

"What do you mean?"

"It's him," Alexander said, looking at Eric.

"Him? Who, the guy in black?"

At that moment, a small man in a pale blue suit walked around the corner and headed towards them. Alexander flinched and quickly closed the locket. He lifted it as if to pocket it in his coveralls, but then hurriedly pressed it into Eric's hands instead.

Eric instinctively slid it into his jeans.

"Here you are," said the small man, a note of disapproval in his voice. "There's a job on the main floor. One of the air-conditioning vents is clogged. It's all these damn power outages. You weren't at your work station."

"I'm terribly sorry," said Alexander. "I'll tend to it now." His stoop was more pronounced now, his voice suddenly deferential.

"Right now," said the supervisor. "It's an emergency. And who's this?" His eyes flicked over Eric.

"My grandson," Alexander mumbled.

The supervisor scowled, and did not look entirely convinced. "Next time, make sure he wears a security pass."

"Yes, I will."

"I'll show him out."

Alexander turned to go, but his green eyes met Eric's for a split second. Eric shivered and looked away. His hand brushed the concealed locket. He'd taken the bait again.

6

Tower of Babel

"He's been watching me."

"This guy's scary," said Chris. "Intensely scary. If I thought some dusty sixty-year-old was spying on me, I'd leave town! Why'd you let him hand you the locket like that? That was dumb."

"I know, I know," Eric sighed. He'd eagerly taken it, though, happy to have it for a little while longer, to touch the smooth old wood, to look at the miniature inside. But he knew it was only being used as the bait on a hook.

He shifted uncomfortably in the skeletal chrome armchair. He'd never liked Chris's apartment. The vast living room reminded him of a very expensive furniture store, sparse and cold. The walls were a blinding white, without paintings or prints, and the furniture was carefully arranged in small clumps, as if on display: two spindly metallic armchairs, a black leather sofa, a white leather sofa, a set of gleaming glass-and-steel shelves that held a stack of matte-black stereo equipment and a huge television, a coffee table made of a slab of ebony balanced on ivory obelisks. A few Japanese vases with dried flowers were placed discreetly around the room. The only things out of place were Chris's designer sneakers, kicked off onto the shining checkerboard-tile floor.

On television, a man was gobbling burning cigarettes, spitting them out, lighting more, then gobbling them up too, until he had twelve smouldering in his mouth at once. Eric felt a sick stirring in his stomach.

"Amazing!" Chris said. "I've never seen anyone do that."

"How can you watch this crap?" Eric said impatiently.

"It's good," Chris protested. "You try smoking twelve cigarettes at the same time."

Eric took a deep breath.

"All right, okay," Chris said, touching the remote-control. The volume faded to a distant roar. "So what're you going to do? I wouldn't go back."

"Why do you think he's been watching me?" Eric said. He twisted in the armchair, trying to find a comfortable position. There wasn't one.

Chris shrugged. "Maybe he's crazy. Maybe he's some kind of pervert who likes little boys. You shouldn't have told him so much about yourself. You told him where you live!"

"He knew anyway," Eric said. "I'm sure of it. A lot of the time it was as if he knew the answers to all his own questions, and was just making me talk."

"He's a psycho."

"No." Eric shook his head. There was something almost familiar about Alexander, something Eric understood. Alexander was like Eric's father in some ways: the old-fashioned words, the snatches of poetry, the things he said about the city.

"Saying love poetry to a picture in a locket!" Chris scoffed. "Sounds pretty crazy to me."

Eric sagged in the armchair. He remembered Alexander snatching the locket from his hands, desperate to have it back. But was that so hard to understand? He hadn't wanted to part with it himself. Maybe Alexander just felt the same attraction, only much stronger.

"It was like it belonged to him," Eric said. "Like he owned it."

61

"I thought you said it came from the museum."

"But the way he held it and looked at the picture—" Eric hesitated as the thought slithered into his head, almost didn't say it. "It was as if he knew her."

"Right," Chris said jeeringly. "Like those old guys who look at skin magazines at the back of the corner store."

"That's not the way he was looking at it, you moron." Eric could feel his face go red. He, too, had spent a lot of time looking at the portrait. Nothing abnormal about that, right? There was just something about her, something mysterious. He wondered if his father ever looked at his old pictures the same way.

"*Me* a moron?" Chris exclaimed. "You're the moron. The woman in the portrait's been dead five hundred years or something and you say that this guy knew her. Right!"

"It was just the way he looked, that's all," Eric said sharply.

"Yeah, because he's crazy. He probably ripped this thing off. Why else would he hide it when his boss showed up?"

"Maybe, maybe." Eric said. He felt suddenly deflated. The same question had stalked through his head. He supposed it was possible for Alexander to have stolen the locket, but Eric just couldn't see him doing it. He'd worked at the museum for years, and obviously loved it. He seemed about as likely a criminal as Eric's father. But it was impossible to know what people were really like. Everyone hid things.

"Well," said Chris, "if you ask me, this thing has ILLE-GAL written all over it in big red letters."

"He wants me to go back," said Eric. "That's the only reason he gave me the locket. He could've hidden it himself just as easily."

"Just ditch it," Chris advised, stretching his muscular arms above his head. "He's crazy."

"But why's he been watching me?" Eric exclaimed. "There's got to be a reason! Why does he want me to go back to see him?"

Chris shrugged, and his eyes strayed to the television.

"Hang on a second."

He touched the remote-control unit and the volume soared.

A curvaceous young woman in a bikini was modelling a new wristwatch TV, whispering guarantees with her wide, crayon-red mouth. All her beautiful friends wore wristwatch televisions, too. They were stretched out on the sand behind her, eyes glued to the miniature screens. They managed to tear themselves away long enough to smile at the camera before the commercial ended.

"Wouldn't one of those be amazing?" Chris said.

"Great," Eric said curtly. Chris was getting as bad as his father, always distracted. No one paid attention anymore. At least Alexander had listened.

"The screen on those things is incredibly thin," Chris was saying.

"A real breakthrough," Eric said.

"Sorry, I forgot I was talking to a techno-peasant."

"Fortunately I can think without the television on."

"Isn't there an encyclopedia you should be reading?"

"Old joke, Chris. And you probably don't even know what an encyclopedia looks like."

"Yeah, well, we can't all be skinny geek geniuses like you, Mr. Superior Intellect," Chris said, cuttingly.

Eric felt a hot flush of guilt. It was true, he liked to feel smarter than Chris. He wondered if Chris knew how jealous he really was—of Chris's popularity, his muscles. Eric could hardly admit it to himself.

"Forget it," he mumbled, wrenching himself out of the armchair. The gleaming white room suddenly made him feel claustrophobic, and he moved to open the glass balcony doors. Hot air crashed into the chill of the air-conditioned apartment. He gazed out over the vast, hazy city. From this height, it looked strange and unfamiliar to him, as though everything were on an angle, crazily tilted.

Chris stepped out to join him and they stood in silence for a few minutes.

"He's not a repairman," Eric said. "I mean, he works as one, but it's like some kind of act."

"So who is he then?" Chris asked doubtfully.

"I don't know. He's terrified of something though. When the lights went out the second time he looked really horrible; he was shaking. And he said it was the guy in black."

"He never said that," Chris corrected him. "You said he didn't have time to answer."

"But I'm sure that's who he meant," Eric said impatiently. The heat pounded against face, seemed to steal away his breath.

"How could this other guy control the electricity?" replied Chris. "Doesn't make sense. Your buddy's intensely crazy."

"What's Alexander hiding from him?" Eric said distractedly. He pushed his hair away from his damp forehead. "If I went back, I could maybe find out."

"Oh, geez," muttered Chris. "Listen, why don't you tell your Dad? See what he says."

Eric snorted. "Dad's been too tired lately," he said unhappily. "He sleeps most of the time he's not on shift."

"Hey, that reminds me; there was something I was going to show you. This'll cheer you up."

Eric squinted into the sky. "Is this thing ever going to break?"

"It's the blueprints for the new mall," Chris explained. "Mom left on her latest business trip without the diskette."

A detailed technical diagram glowed on the computer screen: a tight, geometrical weave of green lines and symbols.

"Hmmm," Eric said. Why was Chris showing him this? Eric wasn't interested in the new mall, and Chris knew that.

"This is the good part," Chris said.

He touched the keyboard and a section of the diagram enlarged to fill the screen.

"This is where we were the other day. When we went down that manhole."

"Really?" Eric leaned in closer to the screen, trying to decipher the electronic maze. Chris manoeuvred a blinking red triangle to a spot on the blueprint.

"That's the manhole, and this is the tunnel, and this must be the platform thing we got to."

"This is really neat," Eric said, and then curbed the enthusiasm in his voice. He didn't want Chris to know he was impressed. But he admired the way his friend's broad fingers travelled deftly over the keyboard while his eyes remained fixed on the monitor.

"Intense, huh?" Chris said.

"Does it show what's down there?" Eric wanted to know.

"Not on this one. But maybe ..."

Chris flashed a series of maps onto the screen until he found the one he was looking for.

"I think this is as deep as it goes. Hang on." He punched a couple of keys and the first diagram they'd looked at reappeared in red, superimposed over the second.

Eric peered into the screen. "So we were standing here, right? Where's the subway tunnel?"

"Can't see it on this map. It runs almost underneath the mall. I was looking at it earlier. It's not far down. Only a couple of storeys: three, maybe four. Amazing thing is, everything's connected down there—the subway tunnels, the manhole shafts, the storm drains, the sewers."

Eric's eyes moved carefully over the map.

"That must be the foundation of the museum, over there," he said, pointing.

"Uh-huh. It's deep as hell," Chris muttered.

"That's what Alexander said. Can you make that part bigger?"

Chris's fingers flew over the keys and the map re-drew itself on the screen.

"Goes down twenty storeys," Chris said.

"He wasn't lying, then," Eric said. "Remember, he was telling me about the storage rooms, and the two empty floors at the very bottom."

"The main storm drain is down there," Chris said, peering at the monitor. "It runs right alongside the base of the museum wall."

"So we were standing right over that," said Eric.

"Yep. It's like a big canyon. A concrete canyon with a river running through it."

"A dried-up river," Eric corrected him. He thought of Jonah, yelling down the grate, throwing his fishing rod to the ground. Clank, clank, clank. He'd heard it, too, the grinding of machinery, seen the spark of light, smelled the dense smoke. Whatever it was down there, it had to be right on the shore of the storm drain. He imagined a monstrous engine, spewing out flames like a dragon, burning away all the water.

"What do you think it was we heard down there?"

"You mean *smelled* down there," Chris snorted. "My nose is still recovering. I don't know what it was. Don't really care. And no, I don't want to go down and have another look." He smiled. "Strung up that little idea, didn't I?"

"Why not?" Eric said.

Chris flicked a switch on the computer and the diagrams disappeared from the screen.

"Well, one very good reason is that it's sealed up. I was by there today, and they've closed it."

"Jonah didn't think it was normal."

"The guy who fishes through the grate?" Chris said with a smirk. "You've been listening to crazy people too much lately. It'll get you into trouble."

Eric followed Chris back to the living room. They were greeted by a barrage of commercials on the television. People jumped out of airplanes holding bottles of beer, a Greek statue came to life to use a razor, the new mall glittered in artificial sunlight, and the Sphinx stood after thousands of years and ate a superior brand of cat food from an enormous bowl.

"How do they make it look so good?" Chris asked, mystified. "*I'd* eat it, it looks so good!"

Eric shook his head in revulsion. But his thoughts were circling back to his meeting with Alexander. Everything had seemed so predetermined—every question, every comment. Why?

"It was as if Alexander was studying me."

But Chris was gone. "Know what I really want?" he said, watching another ad. "A micro cell phone. One of those miniature ones you just clip to your ear."

It was as if he were speaking another language. And Eric felt a strange twinge of loneliness, as if he and Chris had nothing in common. With Alexander, weird as he was, there seemed to be some reassuring link between them, as if they had things to talk about, things they both understood.

He watched Chris watching the television. The wooden locket was still in his pocket. He could feel it against his leg. He knew he'd go back.

7

Necropolis

Eric leaned over the typewriter and read the last sentence his father had written, almost a week ago: *She did not say goodbye, but it seemed obvious—to both of us—that we would not see each other again.*

Eric looked around the humid living room, taking in the sagging bookshelves, the framed prints on the peeling plaster walls, the two sofas with their faded floral pattern, the dilapidated armchairs, the leaning radiator. She used to sit in this room, he thought. He tried to imagine her, lowering herself into one of the chairs, picking up a book from the coffee table.

For a fleeting moment, the whole house seemed to shudder with her presence. She'd lived here. The books: how many of those were hers? And the vase with the dried flowers in front of the bricked-in fireplace—had that been hers, too? The bursting cushions on the sofa? The rug in the corner? Was every room filled with memories of her?

He wondered what she'd looked like and instinctively felt for the locket. His hand froze. He suddenly understood, as if he'd swiftly pushed through a revolving door in his mind. It wasn't Gabriella della Signatura he'd been interested in. It was his mother.

He vaulted up the stairs two at a time, hesitating a moment in the doorway of his father's room.

Go on, he told himself. She's your mother.

He started with the bookcases, feeling behind each row

with his hand, searching for the photo album he had seen only once, years ago. Nothing. He burrowed through the desk drawers, like a thief searching for valuables. He rifled through the night table. Nothing. He opened the huge clothes trunk. Just looking at the wool sweaters made him hot, and when he turned through them, his skin crawled. He pulled up a chair to inspect the highest shelves of the closet. Nothing. Sweat dampened his back. He scuttled on his belly underneath the bed, like a giant beetle, pushing through stray books and dust-clotted debris.

It wasn't here. Where, then?

He stepped out into the hallway and jumped for the cord handle that hung down from the ceiling. The trap door swung out. He eased the wooden ladder all the way to the floor, latched it, and climbed up.

It was exquisitely hot under the pitched roof. The air burned in his nostrils. A tiny dirt-streaked window in the ceiling let in some light, enough for him to see the cardboard boxes and plastic garbage bags piled up on all sides of the trap door. The boxes were all labelled in neat writing, like museum display cases: Linens, Winter Clothing, LPs, Christmas Decorations. Many were simply labelled with his mother's name, and Eric guessed they held her clothing, jewellery—things his father couldn't bear to get rid of.

Most of the larger boxes were sealed with masking tape. Crouching over, Eric shifted them out of the way to see farther back into the attic. And there, pressed against the eaves, was a smaller box, folded closed, marked Photographs. He dragged it towards the ladder and pulled out the cardboard flaps.

Inside was the photograph album. A few loose pictures slipped from between the pages as he lifted it out of the box. He balanced it on his pointy knees, opened the cover.

There she was.

He brought the album closer to his face, angling it so that the pictures caught more light. She was slender, of medium height, with long, dark hair: nice-looking. In the first picture, she was with Dad, standing by a bridge with tall lamp posts. Trees and old stone buildings lined the far bank of the river. The Eiffel Tower stood in the background, outlined in neon. Dad was looking straight into the camera, smiling, but his mother was looking away at the Eiffel Tower, her face very still and serious, half-turned in profile. Eric felt his skin crawl. It was virtually the same pose as Gabriella della Signatura's.

Underneath the photo, in handwriting he'd never seen before—his mother's, he guessed—it said "City of Light." In the next picture, his mother was standing alone in front of a fountain with a winged statue at its centre. She was smiling, but her eyes were still solemn.

He studied her face carefully, but couldn't see any similarities to his own features. Maybe, he thought bitterly, if he'd looked more like her, Dad would have paid him more attention. Maybe. But he was built like Dad: same narrow bones, same skinny face.

Eric flipped ahead through the album. There were more shots of Paris, and then some back here in the city, in places that he knew. His mother wasn't smiling in most of the pictures; when she was, there was a forced look about it.

Near the back of the album, she was pregnant, getting bigger; then, on a page by itself, was a picture of her, all slim again, a little tired-looking, sitting in the living room, holding a baby in her arms.

That's me, he realized.

He waited for a surge of emotion, but it didn't come. He didn't feel as if he were part of the picture. He didn't have

71

any memory of being held like that. It was him, and yet it wasn't him at all.

In the photo, the living room looked exactly the same as it did now—not a piece of furniture out of place. Dad must have kept it like that on purpose. It wasn't normal. Dad hadn't even tried to forget her. More than that—he was doing all he could to remember. It didn't make any sense, Eric thought. Why remember if it was so painful?

He paged backwards through the album, glanced at the loose photos at the bottom of the box.

His throat tightened. He'd wanted to learn all about her, to get all the answers. But all the photographs in the world couldn't tell him what he longed to know. Idiot, he told himself; you were an idiot to think they would.

He put the album back in the box and left the heat of the attic. There was an empty ache in his stomach. He slid the ladder back up and, with a sudden surge of frustration, slammed the trap door shut. The sound boomed through the house.

"I saw the pictures," he said.

His father nodded. He didn't seem at all surprised, merely tired and defeated. He brushed perspiration from his forehead.

"I don't know why you never showed them to me."

"It was stupid. You have a perfect right to see them. I've done this very badly."

His father fell silent again, and Eric looked across the room at him. The space between them seemed infinite. Eric had hoped that the pictures would bring his Dad back, give them something to talk about.

"Come on," Mr. Sheppard said, rising quickly from the chair, "I'll show you."

"What?" Eric said.

"Come on."

The necropolis sat on a hill overlooking the city. Eric gazed at the dim clutter of tombstones, butting up against one another, many worn and chipped, some split in two. Family crypts had settled askew into the earth. Grave monuments thrust up crookedly from the weeds and wild grass, mirroring the city's skyline.

Eric looked at his father, face pale in the lunar glow of the city. So this is where she's been all these years, he thought.

He squinted at the dates on some of the tombstones as he and his father passed. Many were hundreds of years old, so blackened and eroded that he could barely read the chiselled inscriptions. *Here lies ... In beloved memory of ... Rest in peace.* Everywhere he stepped, it seemed, there was a small grave marker underfoot, with nothing but a name and date cut into it.

"Here," his father said. "It's here."

A few steps more and he stopped at a tombstone, erected recently enough so that it gleamed white in the darkness. Eric leaned closer to read the inscription, the dates, his mother's name.

"I would have come too," he said.

"She haunts me, I think," his father said. "Not a ghost, nothing that spectacular—just insistent thoughts of her and the suffering. Maybe that's all a ghost ever is: memory."

Eric pictured her death, as he had done many times before, like some horrible cartoon played in slow motion. A woman caught in the closing doors of the train, the train

73

starting slowly into the tunnel, speeding up. He winced and blocked out the image.

"We'd been planning on leaving," his father said. "I was going to take you and her out of the city to live somewhere else, someplace where you could fall asleep without the sounds of traffic and television ringing in your ears." He tapped his knuckles thoughtfully against his chin, then shook his head. "I shouldn't have put it off. I waited too long."

"Too long for what? How could you have known she was going to be in an accident? That's crazy."

"I should have known, though."

Eric watched his father run halting fingertips over the tombstone. He felt helpless. All the sentences he was trying to form in his head seemed childish and useless.

"Why can't you forget it a little?" he said after a while.

"It's impossible," his father answered.

"Don't I help at all?" Eric asked quietly.

A low-flying advertising blimp moaned overhead, sending swirling patterns of light across the necropolis.

"The new mall," his father scoffed, wincing at the brightness of the billboard sign. "It's inhuman. They'll want to put a mall here one day. They'll want to dig up the earth and all the bodies and build a new mall."

He fell silent for a few moments.

"Well, I've shown you now," he said.

Eric sniffed derisively. "What? What have you shown me? This?" He waved his hand at the tombstone. "This is nothing! This doesn't tell me anything. *You* have to tell me, Dad!"

"There wasn't an accident," he said, not looking at Eric. "I wanted to make it easier for you. You were too young."

"What do you mean?" Eric croaked, his throat dry.

"She killed herself. She jumped in front of a train."

"Why?" Eric asked after a moment. He felt as if his knees might buckle beneath him.

"She often had long bouts of depression."

"Why?" Eric asked again.

"That's the question that goes on forever. Maybe I should have taken her somewhere better. Maybe I didn't love her well enough."

Eric shook his head in disbelief.

"You let me believe a lie all this time," he said, incredulous.

"I shouldn't even have told you now. It's like a cancer. It just grows and grows. It's impossible to forget."

Eric stared at his father, hating him. Thirteen years and *you've* done everything you can to remember. You don't want to be happy. Won't even try. All you want is your stories and your memories and your dates and your visits to the museum. You don't want me. You lied to me.

"I can't ever forget," his father said. "And I'm worried I'll never forgive her."

The city's electric glare seemed to hollow out his father's cheekbones.

You belong here, Eric thought. City of the dead.

In the dream, Eric was gazing into the locket, studying the portrait of Gabriella della Signatura. The lines of the painting seemed sharper than usual, the colours more vibrant. Light danced off every surface. And then he was no longer simply looking at the picture: he was a part of it. He had somehow been pulled across the threshold of the painting and was now standing in the same room as the young woman.

She sat very still, posing for her portrait. She didn't notice him. Her eyes gleamed challengingly, fixed on something at the far end of the room. Eric tried to turn and look, but couldn't. All he could do was look straight ahead, but at the edge of his vision he made out the hazy shape of a standing human figure. He tried to wrench his head to the left, but it was no use.

He felt panic rising. Who was there? The figure stood motionless. He tried to call out, but he had no voice. He looked back at Gabriella. Her gaze was unbroken, intent and passionate. He looked out through the arched windows to the landscape beyond, and then all at once, though he wasn't aware of moving, he was outside.

Gone were the rolling hills, the church spires, the sea. A scorched desert stretched before him, the throbbing sun close to the horizon. The light hurt his eyes. There was Jonah up ahead with his fishing rod, casting his line out into the sand dunes.

He won't catch anything, Eric thought. That's the stupidest thing I've ever seen. Can't catch fish in the desert.

Then he realized he wasn't alone. Alexander was walking alongside him.

"Did you know her?" Eric asked, turning to look up at Alexander, but unable to see his face, because it was veiled in shadows. When the shadows cleared, Eric saw that Alexander's face was swarming with flies, collapsing, his skin sinking around his cheekbones, sand blowing into the empty eye sockets, the gaping mouth.

Eric woke with a start. It took him a few moments to catch his breath. Just a dream, only a dream. He saw light coming from outside his door and knew that his father must be awake. He turned over and shut his eyes. Tomorrow he'd take the locket back for good.

8

Speaker of a
Dead Language

"You're like me," Alexander said. He appeared without warning at Eric's side, in the dinosaur gallery. "Yes, much like me."

"What do you mean?" Eric kept on walking and fought
back a shudder, watching Alexander from the corner of his
eye. That musty smell permeated the air, stronger than
before. It made Eric think of very old things, ancient ruins
lost in desert sand.

"That's how I knew," Alexander hurried on. "I was
certain I was correct. I've observed you over the years—the
innumerable visits you made here with your father, all the
scribbled entries in your notebooks. How many have you
filled now over the years? Three, four?"

"Four," Eric said.

"I've seen your eyes, filled with awe. And that morning
in the medieval gallery, when the armoured soldier was
knocked over—I saw you flinch, almost cry out, as if stung.
What was it that appalled you so?"

"I brought you your locket," Eric said perfunctorily. He
didn't want to hear any more. He wanted only to get rid of
the locket and leave the museum.

"I'll tell you what it is," Alexander went on, brushing
flecks of dry skin from his thick eyebrows. "You love the
past; you crave it like an opiate, an elixir, a drug." He had
lowered his voice to a whisper and leaned closer, as if shar-
ing a secret. "You understand its beauty and its power."

"Why have you been watching me?" Eric demanded. He stopped in the corridor and faced Alexander. He wasn't frightened anymore; he was too angry. And he was tired of secrets, tired of people hiding things from him.

"It's being consumed, Eric. Here, in the city, all around us, the past is being demolished and burned. This place is one of the last strongholds, here in the galleries, in the workrooms and storerooms. You don't want to see it vanish, do you?"

"I don't know what you're talking about," Eric snapped.

"You have only to look at the new buildings heaving themselves out of the earth—look no further than the building across the path, the new shopping mall," Alexander said. "You have only to look at the moving pictures of the television to see the world speeding away from the past at a horrifying rate. Look at the fires—at the library and the antiques dealership."

He sounded alarmingly like Eric's father. Eric wasn't interested in any of it anymore. Not his father, not the locket, not the museum. None of it.

He pulled out the locket, feeling only the tiniest tug at his heart as Alexander's hand swooped down like a bird of prey to seize it.

"Good, good," Alexander said. "You're most trustworthy, as I thought." He pried the locket open hurriedly, as if to make sure the portrait was still there.

"Did you steal it?" Eric wanted to know.

"Oh no, no. It's mine—a family heirloom."

"Who was she?" Eric heard himself ask.

"Gabriella della Signatura," Alexander replied softly, still gazing at the locket. "The third daughter of a wealthy Venetian spice merchant, and an unrivalled beauty. There were more than a hundred suitors, from as far away as the

British Isles, vying for her hand—or so it was said. She wanted none of them. But her parents eventually betrothed her to Giovanni Braccio, a Florentine prince. She died before the nuptial mass—a sudden fever that took her swiftly."

Eric watched Alexander's face in amazement. It was filled with the same longing and remorse Eric had seen on his father's face as they had stood looking at the tombstone.

As if he knew her.

There it was again, that same thought, slithering through his head.

"She has a mesmerizing face, doesn't she?" said Alexander sadly. "So vital still after these five centuries." He brushed the portrait gently with one finger.

A segment of the dream he'd had the night before played itself out in Eric's head like a stuttering, grainy image on a TV screen: the room, Gabriella della Signatura, the windows, and someone at the very edge of the picture. Who?

Alexander closed the locket and slipped it into his coveralls before looking down at Eric. "I knew you wouldn't fail me," he said.

"It was all some kind of test, wasn't it?" Eric said warily. "What if I hadn't brought it back?"

The suggestion of a smile passed across Alexander's wrinkled mouth, but his expression quickly turned into a grotesque grimace as a cough tore through his chest and throat. A dream image flared in Eric's mind—Alexander's face, his flesh and bone, caving in, disintegrating.

"No," Alexander said after the coughing had calmed to an asthmatic wheeze. "That was never a possibility. I've been observing you. I knew it would bring you back. I am well acquainted with the effect the past has on people. It's like gunpowder in their veins; they can't stop thinking about it."

Just like Dad, Eric thought—obsessed by her death. Suicide. It was worse than an accident, worse than any other kind of dying. As dead as you could ever be. A shapeless anger stirred inside him; he hated his father for telling him something so terrible and, at the same time, for hiding it for so long. He hated his father for not forgetting—not even wanting to. Hated him for not loving him enough.

He glared up at Alexander. "Why have you been watching me?" he demanded, his voice rising. "What for?"

A knot of visitors was making its way through the gallery, and Alexander waited a few moments before he replied.

"To see if you could be trusted," he said in a hoarse whisper.

"Trusted for what?"

"There's something—"

The lights flickered, like candle flames in a gentle breeze. Eric felt a ghostly prickle of sweat across his back.

Alexander's eyes darkened, sweeping across the ceiling, as if he expected one of the pterodactyls suspended there to come swooping down upon them.

Another winking of the lights.

"The man in the armoury?" Eric said.

"Yes."

"Who is he?"

"An old acquaintance."

"And he's making the lights do this?" Eric asked, and was surprised at the skepticism in his voice. He sounded like Chris. "How?"

Alexander waved his hand dismissively. "He has a mastery of machines. He can control them. Electricity!" He said the word contemptuously. "That is his strength. He understands machinery. I do not."

"So what does he want?" Eric asked.

"Something very ancient," Alexander said. "And very valuable. " His voice gained urgency. "He'll try to steal it. But if you were to take it away for a while, like the locket, just like the locket, and keep it safe—"

"Why don't you call the police, if you're so worried?" Eric cut him off, belligerent. So that was it: Alexander wanted to use him. Maybe Chris was right; maybe there *was* something illegal about it all. Well, he'd had enough; he was sick of the cryptic answers he kept getting to his questions— when they were answered at all. He wasn't going to be used like a fool.

"The police would be of no assistance," Alexander said darkly. "Were they able to prevent the last two conflagrations?"

Eric felt suddenly lightheaded; everything seemed to shift sharply to the right. He touched the railing for support. A chunk of memory plunged from the ceiling of his mind: the words of the man in black. *Flames are best for old things ... They burn so easily. They didn't have what I was looking for, so ...* The fires at the rare-book library and at the antiques dealership!

"He set them?" Eric gasped.

"Those aren't the only two," Alexander said quietly. "There have been others, many others."

Eric took a step back from Alexander.

"Who are you really?" he asked, panic flapping through his insides. "You aren't really a museum worker, are you?"

"Will you take it?"

"I don't know you."

81

"Yes, you do," said Alexander insistently. "You're like me."

Eric was enveloped in Alexander's thick, dusty smell. He thought he was going to choke. He looked into Alexander's face, saw the deeply etched lines around his eyes and nose and mouth, the vertical furrows gouged into his gaunt cheeks, like dark grooves in ancient clay.

"You don't want to see all this burn, do you?" he said urgently. "You love the museum. You feel as I do. Outside these walls, the past is being demolished. You've seen it with your own eyes. We must protect it—all this, all that I've struggled for centuries to achieve."

They stared into each other's eyes.

Eric was afraid to move. He pictured the inside of his head as a tumultuous ocean suddenly gone mirror-smooth. It all made sense, as if he'd half-known all along.

"You knew her," was the first thing he could say.

Alexander hesitated for only a moment, then: "Yes."

"It's you she's looking at," Eric said. "You were standing there when it was painted."

"Yes." The word came out as a weary sigh.

Eric made the calculation quickly. He felt absurdly calm. Some part of him was vaguely aware that he should be incredulous, should be gasping in disbelief. He wasn't. Dates his father had taught him surfaced silently in his mind: Methuselah, 969 years old; Noah, 950.

Yet he was trembling as the next question itched the inside of his mouth.

"How old?" he said. "How old are you?"

Alexander touched his hands to his face. " 'Devouring Time, blunt thou the lion's paws,' " he muttered to himself, and laughed. He looked back at Eric. "The invention of photography."

"1827," Eric answered immediately. "Niepce's photographs on a metal plate. But you must be older—"

"The Battle of Waterloo."

"1815." It was the familiar game.

"The first French Republic."

"The 1790s; I don't know exactly when."

"That will suffice. Oliver Cromwell's rule in England."

"I don't—"

"1653 to 1658. Michelangelo's paintings on the Sistine ceiling."

"Early 1500s?"

"Yes. The Black Death."

"1330?" His mind was swirling now as Alexander plunged him deeper and deeper into history.

"1346 to 1348. Marco Polo's travels in China."

"Around 1280. Is that when you were—"

"The Crusades," Alexander cut him off.

"Late eleventh and twelfth centuries." Deeper and deeper.

"The Battle of Hastings."

"1066."

"The coronation of Charlemagne."

Eric shook his head.

"800. The fall of the Roman Empire."

"400 A.D."

"There—that's it! 331 Anno Domini."

Eric whistled under his breath, performing the mental arithmetic.

"Sometimes," Alexander said softly, "I can scarcely believe it myself. *Tempus fugit.*"

"Latin," Eric said. "You speak Latin." He found he was thinking very clearly and quickly, suddenly remembering things that had lain dormant at the back of his mind, snatches of conversation from the medieval armoury. "You're Roman, then."

"I was born in Alexandria, the city from which I took my name," the ancient man replied. "It was under Roman jurisdiction, in the weakening Empire. I've never forgotten Latin; my first tongue it was."

He fell silent for a moment, apparently inundated by memory. His eyes narrowed slightly, as if he were trying to make out something far in the distance.

"I've seen so much," he said slowly, almost absentmindedly. Then he turned to Eric and there was a spark dancing in each eye. "I saw the Great Library of Alexandria ablaze as its vast collections disintegrated in flame. I saw the Visigoths riding into Rome on horses like dark thunder. I wandered through the ruins of the Empire, through the new kingdoms of the barbarian tribes. I have passed through history like a nomad."

How? Eric wanted to ask; how did you do it? But Alexander had been silent about his past for so long that now the words poured out like a torrent through a breached dam.

"In Northumbria, I worked at the monastery at Lindisfarne, copying holy texts, illustrating them. I indexed the great monastic libraries of Jarrow, Centula and St. Gall. I was summoned to serve under Charlemagne at his famous scriptorium in the Frankish Empire, where the libraries of Italy and Byzantium were joined in our great halls, and Alcuin of York sat day after day in his workroom, restoring the true text of the Bible.

"At the end of the first millennium, after Charlemagne's Empire had been partitioned and wasted by war, I went on to the Clunaic abbey near Macon. Art treasures from the known world and beyond were being hungrily collected

84

and catalogued. Then it was not long before the rise of the universities, the glorious universities, and the world began to learn again. Paris, Oxford, Padua, Bologna. I taught mathematics, astronomy, philosophy: no one ever knew I spoke with the voice of the past."

Eric understood his strange accent now, a mixture of a hundred different dialects from around the world.

"Later," Alexander went on, "I was employed by the great Medici family in Florence—as an advisor on artistic matters for their burgeoning state. I commissioned Cellini, Giovanni Bologna, Michelangelo. Another age passed away."

He paused briefly. His exuberance seemed to be dying out, and there were traces of sadness in his face. He suddenly began coughing, one hand clenched over his mouth, the other against a pocket of his coveralls, gripping the locket.

"Then I returned to Rome and assisted the Pope in transforming the city into one of the wonders of the modern world, the eternal city: Saint Peter's, San Carlo, St. Ivo—all the great churches rose up under my supervision. On the cusp of the seventeenth century, wanderlust overtook me again and I travelled to new cities, to new museums and libraries in Vienna, Berlin, Madrid, Constantinople, but I returned to France, where revolution marched in the streets of Paris, and the Louvre opened its doors, promising to be one of the greatest museums in all time. I stayed there for almost a hundred years, leaving once when it seemed appropriate I should die, then returning some years later when I'd been forgotten.

"By the turn of this century, it was no longer possible to slough off the skins of identity so easily. Records were becoming much more detailed, and the world was contracting with railroads, motorized carriages and trolleys, telegraphs. I could no longer stay at the Louvre without arousing suspicion, so I travelled across the great ocean. I work here doing repairs to escape notice. Had I applied for a higher position, my history would undoubtedly have been checked. But this way, I pass like a spectre through the museum, watching over it all. It must be protected." Alexander's eyes darted nervously around the room. "Like a fool, I thought I could escape him, but he's found me again."

Eric stared at his sneakers, calmly piecing together the jigsaw pieces in his mind. He looked up at Alexander.

"He was at the Louvre with you, wasn't he? He said something about it in the armoury."

"Yes, he was there."

"He looks so young," Eric murmured. An hour ago he would have sworn the man in black was no more than thirty.

"He is almost as old as I," Alexander said. "We worked together at the Library of Alexandria. His name was Macer, but he has changed it a hundred times through the ages. He calls himself *Coyle* now."

"But how?" Eric asked. "How have you both lived so long?"

"That's the greatest secret of all," Alexander said. "The live-forever machine."

9

The Live-Forever
Machine

The freight elevator plunged them into the depths of the museum. Eric watched the painted numbers on the shaft wall slide slowly by: 3, 4, 5 ...

What did a live-forever machine look like? He imagined a massive apparatus bristling with wires, throbbing with electricity, and his thoughts immediately turned to the machinery he and Chris had heard deep beneath Astrologer's Walk, the jagged splinter of blue light, the billowing black smoke. No, that didn't make any sense. There was no electricity back in 300 A.D., no wires, no steel. So what kind of machine was it?

"I was chief librarian at the Library of Alexandria," said Alexander at his side. "It was a storehouse for the knowledge of the known world, past and present. Under our high ceilings were writings from the Hittites, the Phoenicians, the Etamites. There were pictographs from the ancient Sumerians, writings in Akkadian on clay tablets from Babylon and Assyria, ivory boards covered with old Persian, Meriotic script from the African civilization of Kush."

Eric was beginning to feel slightly unreal, as if he were watching everything through water. *He was there!* He had to keep reciting those words to himself in his head.

"I was translating some Babylonian writings on longevity," Alexander went on. "They spoke of the possibility of living eternally. It is a subject to which every age has turned in fascination and longing. It intrigued me then—nothing more. But shortly afterwards I came across some Phoenician writings on the same subject. I delved into the library's immense collection, looking for more. I translated writings from almost all the ancient civilizations, unable to sleep. It had obsessed me, you see, this idea of immortality."

The elevator cable groaned. The numbers slid by: 7, 8, 9. Eric watched Alexander as he spoke. What was it like to have lived that long? he wondered.

"Coyle was my assistant then," Alexander said. "He helped me find some of the material I needed. He had only a vague idea of my research, and I was careful to tell him as little as possible. He was an exceptional scholar, but we couldn't have been more dissimilar. I was content to sift through the past; he was interested only in the latest learning, the latest achievements. He had visions, you know— wild visions of the future that he said came to him in dreams. He ranted about machinery and inventions that seemed impossible at the time. Who could have known they would prove to be true?"

"The way of the future," Eric mumbled to himself, remembering Coyle's words in the medieval armoury.

"After several years," Alexander went on, "I had collected all the writings I had found on eternal life, collated them, fused them into one text, and painstakingly transcribed it onto one long scroll of parchment. I called it, this one document, the live-forever machine—though, of course, it wasn't really a piece of machinery at all, certainly not by today's definition. But that was the way I thought of it then: an incredible, impossible machine. I half-believed it might work."

So it was just paper. Eric felt a twinge of disappointment.

"Coyle found my working papers one day. He read them, translated them into Latin. Then, one night, he tried what I don't think I would ever have tried myself. He tried to make himself immortal. It worked."

"How, though?" Eric asked.

"How is one made immortal?" Alexander hesitated. "It would seem like madness to you. At night, under the eye of the moon, there are certain rituals that must be observed, incantations read aloud. But that is the least of it. When that is done, the person must immerse himself in deep water and drown."

"Make yourself drown?" Eric cried out. "Can you even *do* that?"

"It's the hardest thing in the world, to breathe water willingly into your lungs, to feel them icily fill, to hear your own breath leave your body in choking gasps. But yes, it is possible, by force of will, if you believe strongly enough."

"What happens then?" Eric felt his chest tighten, as if his own lungs were being filled with water.

"You die. For three days, your body settles heavily on the bottom. But then there is the second awakening. You feel yourself stir, as from a drugged sleep. You strain to reach the surface of the water, and you pull yourself out onto the shore. You've become immortal."

The elevator settled with a thud at the bottom of the shaft. The massive doors split apart and Alexander strode out into the harsh fluorescent light, down a long corridor lined with doors. Storage rooms.

"How did you know Coyle had done it?" Eric asked. "How could you tell?"

"It was his eyes," explained Alexander. "They had changed colour. The next morning, when I saw his face, I knew he had done it. He told me, too, laughing, and then I smelled the fire. It spread so quickly that there was no time to stop it. Now that he was immortal, he wanted to destroy the very mechanism of his creation. He wanted to be the only one. What he didn't know—not for hundreds of years—was that I had hidden the complete live-forever machine elsewhere for safekeeping."

Eric glanced through a tiny glass window in one of the storage-room doors. All he could make out were the hard lines and corners of sealed boxes and crates. He shivered. There was something eerie about it, like a room with all the furniture covered over with sheets, dead.

"Looking at Coyle's face that morning, I realized what an evil thing had been born. He laughed contemptuously as the library burned and toppled. It gave him tremendous pleasure. He told me that only by laying waste to the past could he attain his dreamed-of future. Then he fled, and that was the last I saw of him for nearly three centuries.

"I felt as if the contents of Pandora's box had been loosed on the world for a second time. Something had to be done. I feared that he would desecrate everything old that came within his reach. There had to be balance. So that night, I too turned myself immortal with the live-forever machine, and I left Alexandria forever."

At the end of the corridor was a small door, secured by deadbolts and a steel bar. From one of the pockets in his coveralls, Alexander produced a large ring bristling with keys. After opening the locks, he slid the rusting metal beam to one side.

The door swung open into darkness. A warm, fetid wind hit Eric in the face, making his nostrils and throat contract in revulsion. Alexander reached around through the doorway and pulled out an oil lantern. He lit it.

"Watch your footing," Alexander warned him.

Eric looked dubiously at the wooden staircase, rotted by dampness, some steps missing altogether.

"'Each day we take another step to hell,'" Alexander intoned. "'Descending through the stench, unhorrified ...'"

The stairs were built down against the four walls of a square shaft, slanting into darkness.

"I wandered through the ruins of the Empire," Alexander continued. "I collected things that would have been lost forever in the chaos and hid them in secret places in wait for a more stable time. I tried to compensate for what had been lost in the library fire. Moreover, every object I ferreted away was one thing less for Coyle to destroy, one thing more that would survive the ages."

"What did Coyle do after he left Alexandria?" Eric was trying to breathe through his mouth so he wouldn't smell the stale stench of the cellars.

"He became a marauder. I would hear rumours of monastery libraries mysteriously burned to the ground, or castle keeps plundered. What he didn't destroy, he hoarded and sold years later for enormous profits. He'd become very wealthy by the time I met him again.

"He didn't recognize me at first. I had to call him by his birth name, speak of Alexandria and the library. Then he remembered. How he paled! He thought I was a ghost! But he slowly came to realize there must have been another copy of the live-forever machine."

They reached a landing with a door, but Alexander hurried Eric past it.

"I told him that he had destroyed only my working papers in the fire. I told him as well that he had missed one very important piece of the machine—the mechanism that enables a person to unmake himself or others. I warned him that if he did not cease his wanton destruction, I would cast him into the abyss of time."

"Could you really do that?" Eric asked. His mind was beginning to cloud. It was too much all at once, too much to keep straight.

"Yes. If you drown a second time, you are unmade."

"That's it?"

"No, it's not that simple. It must be done beneath the same moon under which you made yourself immortal."

"What do you mean, the same moon?"

"I mean within the same three-day period of the yearly lunar cycle."

"Did you try to unmake him then?"

Alexander was silent for a moment, casting his gaze down to the sodden wooden steps. "No," he said awkwardly. "The time was not right, and he fled immediately.

"Several centuries streamed by before I saw him again. He tracked me to Charlemagne's scriptorium and tried to steal the live-forever machine. He wanted the secret of unmaking so he could do away with me. The scroll was well hidden, but in his anger he cut a swath of destruction through the library's vaults. The three days when I could have unmade him had passed. From then on, he dogged my steps around the world, heedless of my warning. I suppose he thought my threat had been an idle one.

"The most curious thing about Coyle was that he was vastly changed each time I saw him. He was so obsessed with his vision of the future that he would forget everything about the last age in which he had lived: the language, the customs, the knowledge. He was a perfect chameleon. Every year, it seemed, he would learn everything anew. Scarcely a fragment of the past clung to his consciousness except the memory of the live-forever machine, and his drive to unmake me."

They had reached a high door at the bottom of the rotting staircase. Alexander fumbled in his coveralls for his ring of keys.

"The last time I saw him before now was at the Louvre. I trapped him in one of great galleries, and had him taken down to one of the dungeon vaults that hadn't been used since the building's days as a royal residence. I sealed him in, hoping never to see him again. He must have remained there for the better part of a century, smouldering with hatred in the dark. I have no idea how he finally got out. Perhaps an unwitting labourer released him. Now he has come back into the world."

Alexander turned the key in the lock and pushed the door wide open.

"Go in—go," he said.

Eric gasped.

Pirate's treasure, toy shop, art gallery, museum, junkyard. The lantern's light played across smooth marble busts and crude clay statuettes, the canvases of oil paintings, a stone sarcophagus inlaid with lapis lazuli and red limestone, teetering piles of books, a Bull's head plated in gold, a bronze helmet. It was all stacked up against the walls of the cave-like chamber, covering antique tables and bureaus, sprawled out across the floor on Persian rugs. Trunks and strongboxes lay open, filled to the brink with fabulous baubles.

"This isn't part of the museum's collection, is it?" Eric said.

"Oh no," said Alexander, shaking his head. "No, this is mine. My private collection, things I have gathered through time. No one sees these but me. And now you."

Eric no longer noticed the rank smell of the cellars. He felt suddenly like a child again, going through the museum for the first time. There was so much to see here, so many wonderful things. His eyes slipped over the vast array: tapered storage jars, an ivory horn, a jewel-encrusted clock, dagger blades, a silver ladle with a dolphin handle, a stone oil lamp. He wanted to hold them all. He paused at an ornate mechanical hen with a wind-up key in its side, reached out to touch it.

"No!" Alexander shouted, and Eric snatched back his hand.

"Sorry," he replied automatically.

"Don't touch anything," Alexander said, and there was a fanatical glint in his eyes. "Please don't touch anything here."

Eric rammed his hands into his pockets. These things were centuries old. Alexander didn't want them hurt. Made perfect sense.

But as he moved through the subterranean museum, looking more closely, he began to notice the decay. Ancient cobwebs trailed from the damp walls. A ghostly film of dust had settled over everything. Tarnish had coated pieces of metalwork. Some of the books scattered across the floor were wet, and the bindings looked as if they'd been gnawed at.

He heard a rustling sound, and turned quickly to see a rat's tail disappearing into one of the mounds of artifacts.

Eric looked to see if Alexander had noticed.

He was gently brushing dust from a Greek statuette, mumbling to himself.

"*Pro memoria*," he said.

Eric silently watched Alexander, surrounded by his Aladdin's treasure. He wondered if the man was a little crazy. What would it be like to live that long. It was almost impossible to imagine. What would it do to you, knowing that you would never die? You wouldn't think the same way as regular people. It would change the whole way you thought, wouldn't it?

Alexander seemed to have forgotten there was anyone else in the room. He turned to an oil painting of a man in a brilliant red turban.

"*In perpetuum.*"

Alexander was letting his bony fingers trail across the heavy parchment of an open book.

"*Semper idem,*" he intoned.

Eric suddenly thought of their own living room, unchanged for thirteen years. Always the same. Anger flickered inside him. Dad kept everything the same so he'd never forget her.

Alexander stooped to pick up a brass medallion from the floor and polished it against his coveralls.

"You're right on the main storm drain," Eric told him. "That's why it's so wet here."

Alexander started at the sound of Eric's voice.

"Yes, yes, I realize that," he said, turning. "It's not an ideal location—no, by no means ideal—but it's the safest I could find, and these things must stay hidden." He cast a possessive eye around the chamber. "No one must see them. And *he* musn't find it."

There was something almost grotesque about this massive hoard. Why wouldn't someone like Alexander take better care of these things? He loved these things. Why would he put them in a damp cellar? It was crazy.

"Now," said Alexander. "Let me show you."

He made his way back towards a far corner of the room, where there was a huge wooden bureau covered with elaborate carvings and more drawers and cupboards than Eric had ever seen. He watched as Alexander selected a key from his ring, unlocked a narrow set of doors and reached deep inside the bureau. He could hear the sounds of latches being released, unoiled hinges faintly squeaking.

When Alexander drew back his arm, he held a long white canister with a leather handle at one end.

"It has never been opened," he said. "It was sealed without air, to keep the parchment from disintegrating. It's as immortal as the secret it holds. Our lunar cycle is fast approaching," he went on, and there was a hint of hysteria in his hoarse voice. "If he steals the machine, he will discover the secret of unmaking, and it will be the perfect time. I am at my most vulnerable. Take it."

"I don't get it," Eric said. "You can unmake *him* then, too."

Alexander turned away and was silent for a long time.

"You can't imagine the loneliness of centuries," he said, dusting his fingertips over a marble bust.

"For more than sixteen hundred years I've watched those around me fall under Time's scythe while I remain unchanged. I made a promise never to reveal my secret, and I learned to distance myself from people, not to draw too near, not to rely on them. Only once did I lapse."

"Gabriella della Signatura," Eric said, almost without thinking. "She knew."

"Yes. I was foolish enough to fall in love with her. It's ridiculous, is it not—a man of a thousand, falling in love with a girl who had barely reached her twentieth year?"

Alexander's voice had a bitter sting to it. Eric took a few awkward steps around the huge chamber, waiting for him to go on. He felt a tightening in his stomach, and had a sudden mental flash of his father sitting slouched on the sofa at home, brooding about her.

"Did you know that I even offered her immortality? Doubly foolish was I. I'm not sure if she ever believed my story, but she refused. The arrogance of her! She allowed me only to have her painted in miniature. That, she said, would have to suffice for eternity."

Eric thought of the explosive defiance in her eyes, and understood now. It was as if she'd been saying, Look! Look at me! How can you not believe I'll be beautiful and young forever!

"She could have had true immortality," Alexander said. "But she spurned it. She succumbed to fever. I will never forgive her."

Eric winced. His father's words.

"All are snatched away," Alexander said. "Coyle is the only one keeping pace with me through time, my only companion. Sometimes ... sometimes I think I must be mad or that I'm dreaming it all—he is my only proof that I'm sane, do you see? I couldn't unmake him."

"But he'd unmake you!"

"Oh, yes, he would, but I cannot do the same to him. I will not. It would be unforgivable. He is as venerable as these things around us. Coyle is like me, a living artifact."

Eric looked away in confusion and disgust. How could Alexander feel any kind of kinship with Coyle—someone who would eagerly kill him? Like Dad, he thought, you'll cling and cling until it destroys you. Pathetic.

"Will you take it, Eric?"

"You should ask my father. He'd do it." Flinging out the words.

"No, no, it's you. You're the one. I've watched you."

"You made a mistake."

"If Coyle takes the scroll, I'll be cast into the abyss of time, and you will watch all this burn. All these things that have given you so much pleasure. What will you be left with?" he scoffed. "Outside these walls, what is there? Flickering televisions with their promises of happiness and wealth, new malls with everything useless under the heavens, towers of steel and glass that blot out the sun. Here, Eric, here there's a whole world. But once Coyle's found the scroll, he'll raze it to the ground." His voice had become frantic, pleading. "The precious past will disintegrate before your eyes."

The precious past, Eric thought acidly. All he could see was his father being pulled down by the past, being suffocated by it: the photographs and the tombstone and the perfect, videotape memories. What good was it when you wasted away in unhappiness, always lonely and dissatisfied and restless, ignoring and hurting the people around you, who might help if only you'd let them? What good was the past?

"You can do it yourself," Eric told him fiercely. "Why should I take it? You've been watching me, studying me like I'm some kind of guinea pig, lying to me. I don't even think you wanted to tell me who you really were. You just wanted to unload this thing on me. Just as long as I'd bring it back. That's all that mattered. You're just using me. And you don't even care, do you? Coyle would kill me for this, wouldn't he? Well, wouldn't he, if he wants it so badly? Maybe it's almost impossible for you to be killed, but it isn't for *me*. Forget it. *You* could do it if you wanted."

"I can't," the ancient librarian said. "It's not possible."

Eric snorted. The anger burned inside him, in his stomach and chest, encircling his heart. He felt suddenly caged in by a decaying junk heap, sickened by the stink of the cellars.

"Look at all this stuff!" he raged. "You're just letting it rot. My father takes better care of his paperbacks! This is just greed! Things that only you're allowed to touch! To hell with it."

"Take it," Alexander said, holding out the canister. "Help me."

Eric felt an unwanted stab of pity. Don't buckle, he cautioned himself.

"Take care of it yourself." He moved towards the doorway. "He'd never find it down here anyway."

10

The City Rises

"No proof," Chris said again.

"You're right," Eric agreed, a little too eagerly. Come on, he thought, convince me, make me believe it was all lies, all made up.

It was already starting to fade a little in his mind. Once he'd left the darkness of the cellars and reached the busy city street, it had all become vaguely unreal, like some prolonged and particularly vivid dream. Alexander, whispering, whispering; the gargantuan, rotting treasure in the damp cellar; the live-forever machine gleaming in its white canister. How could any of that be true once he'd stepped out onto the street? The cars, the people, the noise, the heat. Concentrate on that.

When Chris had dropped by, Eric was glad. He needed to talk it out with someone. Chris had listened, squinting, shaking his head in disbelief. Eric encouraged him, trying to make it all seem as outrageous as possible.

"I mean, he says he's sixteen—almost seventeen hundred years old or whatever it is," Chris said. "But so what? Nice story! What's to stop me from telling you I've been alive for five hundred years?"

"You're right," Eric said again. "It's ridiculous. None of it can be proven."

Chris shifted in the dilapidated armchair. He wasn't used to having Eric agree with him so easily. It made him nervous. He tried again.

"So he's good at history and can list off all these dates. So what? Show me a photo of him in 1905, looking exactly the same. Then maybe I'd think about it."

Eric just nodded, hungrily storing Chris's arguments. Keep going. Don't stop now.

"And this live-forever machine; don't make me laugh! What is it—just some old paper! You didn't even really see it, did you? Hocus-pocus crap!"

"I know, I know," Eric said. "The way he described it, it was like some kind of magic spell." But once again he remembered Alexander's description of breathing water into his lungs, the icy chill deep inside his body, devouring him. No, no, it couldn't be true, Eric told himself fiercely. Things like that just weren't possible.

"It's like I said yesterday," Chris told him. "This thing sounds like a big con job. I bet all that stuff in the cellar is utterly stolen. He's probably been swiping it from the museum for years."

"Probably," Eric said. "He was just making everything up."

But why, then, couldn't Eric stop believing it? He wanted to believe Chris, but he just couldn't. Alexander's ancient smell, his creviced face, all the dates, events and names he had effortlessly recited: all that, Eric supposed, and maybe even the massive hoard in the cellar could be explained away. But his guts wouldn't let him do that. There was a part of him that knew with unshakable certainty that Alexander was telling him the truth. And he'd been trying to shove it out of his mind so he wouldn't have to feel bad about not taking the scroll. And why the hell should he feel bad anyway?

He began walking around the living room, picking up books from the coffee table and sofas, slamming them back onto the shelves. The heat was like a hard-knuckled fist pushing insistently into the centre of his chest.

"What are you doing?" Chris said.

"Cleaning up. This place is a mess." He scowled at the dust that had collected around the legs of the furniture and was suddenly reminded of the cellar, the cobwebs, the clinging moisture, the neglect.

"He just wanted to use me," he said angrily. "He just wanted me to keep the scroll away from Coyle." He shot another paperback into the bookcase. "He didn't even care about how dangerous it might be for me." He saw the *Museums of the World* book on the floor and kicked it contemptuously under the sofa. "All he cares about is himself and his dusty old things—" He cut himself short. He'd forgotten who he was talking about, his father or Alexander.

"Well, forget it," Chris said, watching Eric a little uneasily. "It's finished. You got rid of the locket, so that's it."

"Yeah," Eric said. "Yeah." He slumped into one of the sofas, looked restlessly around the room, and suddenly wanted to be somewhere else. "Why don't we go back to your place?" he suggested. "It's cooler there."

"Sure. What d'you want to do?"

"Maybe we could play computer games or something."

"You hate computer games."

"You could show me that new graphics program your Dad sent you. Or maybe there's something good on TV. This one's too small."

"All right, yeah," Chris said.

"Good." Eric heaved himself up. Maybe he could shut his mind off and refuse to follow through with any of the thoughts. After a while it would dissolve completely, wouldn't it? If he fooled Chris, maybe he could even fool himself.

Someone was yelling on the street outside the house. Eric walked over and pushed aside the blind. On the steps of the museum, a street vendor had drawn a large crowd and was demonstrating a new ice-making machine.

But it wasn't his voice that Eric was hearing.

It was Jonah's. He'd shambled out onto the street and was standing on the fringes of the crowd, pointing and hollering.

"He's the one, him, there!" he proclaimed. "That's him, sure as I'm me."

Eric followed the line of Jonah's outstretched arm and index finger. His eyes passed over the people on the museum steps, some looking at Jonah in bewilderment, others turning away, indifferent and impatient. Then Eric's eyes settled on a man in black jeans and a matching T-shirt at the back of the crowd.

"There, there, there!" Jonah wailed, hurtling his arm forward.

"What's going on?" Chris asked, coming over to the window.

"Jonah's yelling," Eric said softly.

"The crazy guy who fishes? Who's he screaming at?"

Eric pointed across the road. "Chris, that's him. Coyle."

"Him? Really?"

Eric nodded. "I wonder why Jonah's shouting at him like that."

"And he's supposed to be as old as Alexander, huh?" said Chris scathingly. "He only looks about thirty."

"Doesn't mean a thing," Eric said. "That's not the way it works. You're just frozen at the same age—"

"I thought you said you didn't believe any of this!" Chris said.

"I don't know anymore," Eric said impatiently, looking out the window.

Jonah was still raising hell on the sidewalk, and the crowd was getting nervous, breaking up. The ice-cube salesman tried to shoo him away, but Jonah held fast. No one appeared to care about Coyle; no one was looking at him. All eyes were on Jonah. They knew he was crazy. People were laughing at him now. Coyle left the museum steps and started down the street.

"Why'd you keep on agreeing with me?" Chris demanded. "If you believed it all along?"

"Let's follow him," Eric said, letting the blind swing back into place.

"Eric, he's not immortal—"

"Well, maybe we can find out who he really is, then." Eric walked out into the hall, towards the front door. "You don't have to come." Knowing that Chris would, though. He always did.

"Utterly stupid," Chris muttered.

Dazed by the late-afternoon heat, Eric paused outside the house, shielding his eyes.

"Let's stay on this side at least," Chris said, as Eric made to cross the busy road.

They kept well back, following Coyle down the scalding street. From across the road, Eric watched as Coyle gazed intently all around—at the cars and trucks that growled past, the streetlights, the billboards flanking the street. He tilted his head back to look up at the peaks of the skyscrapers. He paused to press all the crosswalk buttons, examine the instant-banking machines. He paused in front of a computer shop, looking at the machinery on display, then went inside.

The street noise swirled in vicious eddies around Eric's ears. For the first time he could remember, he felt overwhelmed by the frenzied movement and colour of the city.

It didn't make any sense to him, the billboard signs flashing the latest news, the lurid window displays. And where did all these people come from, hurtling down the sidewalks with their briefcases?

What on earth did they *do*?

Coyle had reappeared, holding a plastic bag. Further up the street he stopped to peer at a new highrise through the sidewalk hoardings around the construction site. He watched, fascinated, as the huge crane swung round and round, lifting girders and concrete blocks. His hands, Eric noticed, were twitching by his sides. Then he raised his arms and, like the conductor of a symphony, seemed to be urging the construction onwards, hastening the building's rise.

"He's crazy," Chris mumbled. "He's a freaking maniac!"

Suddenly conscious of people watching him, Coyle began walking again. He lingered for a moment in front of a fast-food restaurant, watching the people on the other side of the glass devour their plastic-foam meals.

"Alexander wasn't lying," Eric said. "He's telling the truth, Chris."

Chris groaned. "How do you know?"

"Look at him. He's acting like some kind of tourist. This is all new to him!"

"So?"

"Remember, Alexander said he trapped Coyle in the Louvre, and locked him up for more than a hundred years?"

"Yeah, right," said Chris expectantly.

"He only got out recently—I don't know, say a year or two ago, something like that. So imagine closing your eyes in 1900, and then opening them again to this! All this new machinery and technology! You'd be completely amazed. No wonder Coyle's gawking at everything. Look at him!"

He'd paused in front of a window display of televisions, stacked in a square five across and five high. He stared, riveted, at the glowing screens. Each TV was tuned to the same station, and Eric felt a little dizzy watching the twenty-five identical images move in uncanny unison. A wrecking ball was swinging, slow and heavy, into the side of an old stone building. A section of the wall crumbled and fell, was crumbling and falling, had crumbled and fallen—twenty-five times. A news reporter appeared in the foreground of the picture, talking into the camera.

Eric could hear Coyle's laughter rise above the sound of the traffic. He was laughing at the swirl of dust, the crumbled masonry, the power of the wrecking ball. The way of the future, Eric thought, with a hot chill running along his back.

"I don't know," Chris was saying slowly. "I don't know about this at all." But Eric could tell he was thinking about it, wondering if it could be true.

Coyle suddenly turned and quickened his pace, disappearing into the subway entrance.

"Let's keep up," Eric said, and they dashed across the street, swerving around honking cars. Eric led the way down the subway steps, along the gleaming tiled corridor to the turnstiles, then down again on the dizzyingly steep escalators to the long platform. The heat seemed even more palpable here, with steam rising in broad swaths from the tracks and the darkened tunnel openings. People stood fanning themselves with newspapers and paperback books.

"Where the hell is he?" Chris whispered as they made their way slowly along the platform.

"Nowhere, nowhere," muttered Eric on their second pass. He could feel the column of stifling air being pushed through the tunnel ahead of the oncoming train. He felt the familiar vibration through his feet, heard the growing rumble; then the subway exploded into the station. Out of habit, Eric glanced at the conductor's window, but his father wasn't there.

They stood back to watch as people got on or off the train. No sign of Coyle. The doors snapped shut, the whistle sounded twice, and the train lurched on into the tunnel, leaving in its wake the smell of oil and machinery.

"Lost him," Chris said.

The grit from the tracks swirled up and stung Eric's eyes. He turned away. A drunk teetered perilously at the edge of the platform, and then staggered back. Eric suddenly thought of his mother. Had it happened here, at this very station; had she stood right at the edge of this platform, waiting, waiting? How could you make yourself do it? He watched as the train's rear lights disappeared into the darkness.

11

Two
Storms

Eric watched from his window as the street filled with cruisers and firetrucks.

Red lights swirled in the mid-morning heat. The wail of sirens had given way to the crackle of static from police radios and walkie-talkies. Police officers were cordoning off the sidewalks with thick yellow tape. They started turning back traffic, clearing away the street vendors from the museum steps. An officer was trying to dispatch the hotdog seller, gesturing with his arm. The other man just shrugged and offered him a hot dog. The officer hesitated and then took it.

Two black trucks with c.e.s. stencilled across their sides were allowed through the barricade at the intersection. The trucks' back doors shot up and people in leather armour jumped out.

"City Emergency Services," Eric muttered. What was going on?

They began rolling out heavy equipment, electric generators and pumps, pushing them up to the manhole covers in the middle of the road.

"Okay, let's open 'em up!" one of the men shouted.

The manhole covers were levered up with crowbars and metal ladders were hooked into place. Men wearing oxygen masks climbed down, and machinery was lowered after them.

There was a sharp knock at the front door. Eric started. It was one of the Emergency Services workers, sweat glistening on his broad face. An oxygen mask dangled around his neck, hissing faintly.

"Are you the only person here?" he asked.

Eric nodded. "My Dad's at work."

"We'll have to ask you to leave the premises temporarily," the man said. "There's a gas leak in the vicinity. It's nothing serious. You don't need to take anything with you."

"Right now?"

"Yes."

Eric stepped out onto the street, locking the door behind him. Across the road he could see an arrowhead of uniformed personnel moving up the museum steps against the tide of evacuating visitors and staff. The fire marshal stood at the top, speaking into a walkie-talkie.

"Where's the leak?" Eric asked, but the Emergency Services man was gone.

They were evacuating the highrises on either side of Eric's house, and the sidewalk was now teeming with men and women in business suits, people in dressing gowns with small children, listless teenagers. Eric had never seen any of them before.

A woman with a megaphone was giving directions, but Eric hesitated, watching the museum steps, wondering if he'd catch sight of Alexander. People jostled around him impatiently.

"It's the heat," he heard someone say.

"There was one like this just yesterday," another man said. "Gas line rupturing from the heat."

"I can smell it," a woman said anxiously. "I'm sure I can smell it."

"I can, too," said someone else.

"They say it's coming from the new mall."

"The whole block's going to blow if they don't shut it off."

"I can smell it now, too!"

A ripple of hysteria went through the crowd.

"Cover your face!" someone shouted.

"Is it poisonous?" a worried voice wanted to know.

"Why do you think those guys are wearing masks?"

Eric sniffed the hot air. He couldn't smell a thing. Behind him, a woman screamed and the crowd surged ahead in a spasm of alarm. People were starting to push, and he was swept along in the current, hemmed in on both sides, shoved up against the person in front of him.

"Stay calm," the woman with the megaphone said. "There is no cause for alarm."

"I can't breathe!" someone shouted up ahead.

"It's choking me!"

"Hurry! Run!"

"Please continue to evacuate in an orderly fashion," the woman instructed them.

The crowd wasn't listening. It suddenly occurred to Eric that someone was going to get crushed, and it was probably going to be him. *Skinny Geek Snapped in Two*—he could just see the headlines in tomorrow's papers. Someone grabbed his arm. He yanked it free, an obscenity on the tip of his tongue. It was Chris.

"A little drama, huh?" Chris said, grinning at him. "Just what was missing from our summer holidays."

Eric was so glad to see him.

"This is getting ugly," Eric said, and at the same moment, someone shoved him from behind.

"Hey, take it easy, pal!" Chris shouted, whirling around. He towered over a very anxious-looking businessman. "Give us a little space!"

The businessman hung back and let himself be swallowed up by the crowd.

"About time the muscle showed up," Eric said jokingly, but he meant it. "You hear anything about this leak?"

Chris shrugged. "Everyone's saying something different. All I heard was that one of the underground gas lines is busted. Under the mall maybe."

"Can you smell anything?"

Chris shook his head. "Nah. And neither can they," he told Eric with a wink, nodding to the people around them. "They're flipping out."

A Split Second News van pulled up along the sidewalk. Its side door slid back and a woman with a camera balanced on her shoulder sprang out with cat-like agility, trailing cables behind her. Two men stepped out from the front, and Eric recognized the familiar television face of Stuart Daw.

"First rate," Daw said, nodding appreciatively at the mayhem around him. "Get some shots from here," he told the camerawoman. "All the police cars and stuff, and then all these guys leaving their homes."

A buzz went up through the crowd as various people caught a glimpse of the reporter.

"Look, look, look," some were whispering, nudging their neighbours. "Look, it's the guy from Split Second News, Stuart Daw."

"Where does he get those amazing clothes?" Eric heard a boy behind him whisper.

"He's a great reporter," a woman said with conviction. "And he has a cute smile."

A few teenaged girls actually tried to touch him as they passed, and Stuart Daw smiled and waved.

"Thanks," he said. "Thank you. Please, go on with your evacuation; thanks very much."

Up ahead, the camerawoman was pointing the snout of her camera into the passing crowd. Everyone was jostling to get on TV.

"All right, people," Stuart Daw was shouting, "we're going live in a few seconds! Please don't look at the camera."

Eric smiled cheerfully and waved into the camera as he passed.

Chris choked back laughter. "Amazing," he said.

At the intersection, they passed through the police barricade. A recorded message on an endless loop was being piped over a van's loudspeaker. "The gas leak is not a serious one," the synthesized voice said blandly. "There is no risk of an explosion. We're hard at work and in full control of the situation. In the meantime, please let City Emergency Services take care of everything. The gas leak is ..."

"First thing is to find someplace air-conditioned," said Chris. "This has to be the hottest day ever."

Eric led the way to the twenty-four-hour doughnut store up the street, and they sat down at a mangy booth by the window. A huge, lint-clogged vent in the wall blew icy air over them. Eric tried to mop up some coffee that had coagulated on the table.

"This is utterly gross," said Chris. "If I'd known we were coming here, I would have gotten a tetanus shot."

"Good doughnuts," Eric told him. "Dad sometimes picks up a box on his way home."

He leaned his head against the window and looked down the street towards the museum. There were gas leaks all the time in the city. You heard about them on the news, a house suddenly exploding, leaving nothing behind but a charred skeleton of itself.

112

"You think it's under the new mall?" he asked. "The leak?"

"If it is, Mom's going to freak out. Place is supposed to open in a couple of months."

"You two planning on ordering anything?" the cashier shouted. " 'Cause if you aren't, out of here!"

Eric fished in his pocket for change and Chris went up to the counter to buy a couple of chocolate donuts.

Eric looked back out the window. From the moment he had gotten up that morning, he'd been nagged by guilt, as if some cartoon angel were perched on his shoulder, whispering into his ear. Alexander's face wavered in his mind like a heat mirage, intoning, Help me. Help me. Help me.

Why should I? he argued. What kind of craziness was that, letting the things you were supposed to be taking care of just fall apart? What was the difference between that and Coyle wrecking the soldier statue on purpose? Alexander must be going crazy, Eric thought. Wouldn't anyone? After living for so many years, maybe you'd start to go funny in the head, start doing weird things. A sixteen-hundred-year-old case of senility.

But why the twist of guilt in his own heart then? He watched the police barricade part to let through another C.E.S. truck.

"Here." Chris handed him a doughnut.

The table shuddered as a subway train passed beneath the street. They ate in silence. Eric felt awkward, as if they were both suddenly afraid to talk to each other.

"You still don't believe any of it, do you?"

Chris looked uncomfortable. "I don't know; I can't—it's just not enough, what you've told me."

"So what's your version, then?" Eric asked irritably.

"I told you. Alexander's just stealing this stuff, and maybe

113

he had some deal with Coyle—maybe he owed Coyle for something, I don't know—and he backed out. So now Coyle's come to collect, and Alexander wants to unload it on you."

"And everything Alexander told me about his past?"

"Crap."

Eric rolled his eyes. "Well, that's just brilliant."

"Yeah, well," Chris said defensively. "If you're so utterly sure, why didn't you take the scroll?"

"That's not—" Eric sighed. He didn't know how to explain. It had nothing to do with whether he believed Alexander. He did. But Alexander didn't care what happened to Eric, as long as the live-forever machine was safe. So forget it. If Alexander really loved the museum, he could save it himself by unmaking Coyle. The precious past. He was just like Dad. So go ahead, let it wreck you, let it make it impossible for you to write or talk to your son or be happy. The real answer? He didn't take the scroll because Alexander reminded him of Dad. Try telling that to Chris.

"Forget it," Eric said.

"You haven't told your Dad any of this?"

Eric hunched his bony shoulders.

"Wow," said Chris. "That bad, huh?"

"Dad's a mess," Eric blurted out. "He's distracted all the time, and we don't talk very much. It's just been really awkward. We can hardly wait to leave the dinner table and get away from each other." He paused, checked the anger in his voice. "It's because of Mom."

Chris watched Eric, waiting for him to go on.

"He spends all his time thinking about her," Eric stumbled on. "All those stories he writes—they're about her. He has pictures of her that he never showed me, but I found them a couple of days ago in the attic. When I told him, he took me to the necropolis and showed me where she was buried. He goes there all the time without telling me. He remembers everything about her, Chris. He just thinks and thinks about her. But he never tells me any of it. Thirteen years."

He wanted to tell Chris the truth about his mother, to spill it out. But he couldn't. What would Chris think, that she was insane, selfish, weak? How could he explain why she was depressed? Chris would say his mother took one look at him and threw herself in front of a train. It put a sickening thought in his head. Maybe he did have something to do with her suicide. The timing certainly made it look that way, didn't it? He'd never know. His father sure wasn't going to tell him.

"I don't get why he doesn't talk to you about it," said Chris. "I thought you guys talked about everything. I always thought it was—" he looked awkward for a moment "—kind of cool."

"Well, now you know," Eric said curtly. "It's always been a big wrench in the works."

"Nothing special," Chris said, and Eric was startled by the harshness in his voice. "I mean, my Mom and I hardly ever talk—she's hardly ever home, and even when she is it's always business, business, business. Call the office, drag some work up on the modem, make a few last-minute deals." He snorted. "Always thought you guys had some kind of utterly perfect television life. Quality time and all that garbage."

Eric didn't know what to say. He carefully lined his fingers up on the edge of the table. He'd never thought about Chris's life that much, what happened in his home. He felt disgusted with himself, wallowing like a hippo in self-pity. Like father, like son.

115

"You know what I do?" Chris said. His face had hardened. "It works best this way. I just stop thinking of her as a parent, and think of her as just another person. That way, it doesn't really matter what she does. If she's not around, or whatever."

"Do you miss your Dad a lot?" Eric asked.

Chris rocked his head from side to side, as if thinking it over. "Yep," he said. "Don't know why sometimes, but I do. Good memories, I guess."

Eric nodded thoughtfully. He looked towards the museum. It held a lot of good memories—the dinosaur gallery, the Egyptian mummies, the rooms and rooms of artifacts he'd wandered through with his father over the years. Those things, at least, wouldn't change. But all at once Alexander's words resounded in his head.

You will watch all this burn.

His eyes flickered nervously over the emergency vehicles lined up in front of the museum. Gas leak. Happened all the time.

"They said it was just a small one, right?"

"Huh?" Chris followed Eric's gaze out the window. "Oh, yeah. No big deal. Remember the pipes we saw in the tunnel? They were already kind of leaking. They're utterly ancient."

Another train rumbled by. Eric watched his hands tremble on the shuddering table. And then it all came together in his head.

"He's underground."

"What?"

"Coyle." His mouth had gone dry. "Yesterday, where did he go? He disappeared. He must have gone into the subway tunnels."

"You don't know—"

"It's Coyle," Eric insisted. "He's broken the gas line. He's down there." He could feel the short hairs on the back of his neck tingle. "You said all those tunnels were connected: subway, manhole shafts, storm drains. He's down on the shore of the main storm drain. That's his machinery we heard. 'You reek of machinery.' Alexander said that to him in the armoury. And the smell—Coyle smelled the same as that underground smoke."

"You sure?"

"Jonah must have known all along. That's why he was yelling at Coyle." Eric's heart made a sickening lurch. "He wanted me to tell Alexander. I thought he was just crazy. I didn't even tell him, Chris!"

"Shhh," said Chris, looking around the doughnut shop. "You're freaking everyone out."

"I've got to tell him, at least," Eric said, sliding out of the booth. "He doesn't know." He stumbled out into the heat.

"I don't get it," Chris said behind him, walking fast to keep up. "They've found the leak; they'll close it off. Nothing's going to happen to the museum."

"It's not that," Eric gasped. "Alexander doesn't know he's down there. He's right on the other side of the cellar wall! Where Alexander keeps the scroll! The gas leak was just to get everyone out of the building."

The heat was unbearable. Every ragged breath Eric took burned his lungs. The sky was the colour of lead, the clouds so low they seemed to brush the peaks of the highrises.

"We're not going to get through," Chris said as they neared the police barricade. A large crowd of spectators had gathered at the intersection. Street vendors had set up concession stands and were selling evacuation coffee mugs and T-shirts.

"Now just keep back," said a police officer at the barricade, taking a bite of a hot dog. "There's nothing to see here.

117

Excuse me, sir, you'll have to come down immediately."

Someone with a video camera had climbed up on the roof of a police cruiser to get a better shot.

"Sir, I'm going to have to ask you to come down from there." The man with the video camera didn't budge. The officer shook his head in annoyance and handed his half-eaten hot dog to Eric. "Would you hold this a second, please?" He turned and climbed onto the cruiser.

"Here." Eric plunked the hot dog into someone else's hand. "Come on," he said to Chris, and ducked under the yellow tape. Crouching low, he darted between parked police cars towards a firetruck pulled up along the sidewalk. He could hear Chris's rapid footsteps behind him.

"You're nuts!" he hissed. "The front steps are crawling with cops. We'll never get inside. Let's go back before we get caught."

Eric slumped against the huge wheels of the firetruck. They were out of sight—for a while, anyway.

"There must be some way inside."

A warm drop of water hit him on the forehead. As he looked up, a heavy rain all at once began to fall, clattering against the pavement. The torrent fell against Eric's face, mingling with his sweat, soaking into his shirt, his jeans. He watched, amazed, as a small puddle formed in a shallow depression near his feet.

"I know," he said. "Jonah."

They found Jonah near his storm drain grate on Astrologer's Walk, wrapping himself in plastic garbage bags.

"Batten down the hatches!" he cried out as he lashed another bag around his leg with fishing line. "And take in the sails, for it's God's own wrath this time, you can mark my words."

"You sure about this?" Chris asked suspiciously as they moved closer. "I don't think this guy's brain is fully operational."

"If anyone knows how to get in, he will."

The rain was coming down even harder now, and Eric's clothing clung to his skin. He felt as if he were breathing steam into his lungs.

"You'll catch your death of water," Jonah shouted at them, peering through the plastic hood he'd rigged for himself. He beckoned them with broad sweeps of his arm. "Come here, my Phoenician sailors."

"Oh geez," mumbled Chris.

Jonah was handing them plastic bags and fishing line.

"Is there any way to get inside?" Eric asked awkwardly, pointing at the museum wall.

"The noise it made down there, Ishmael!" he said to Eric. "The crumbling and crashing, the rumbling and roaring!"

"Where?" Eric asked in alarm. "The storm drains?"

"Fire and brimstone!" Jonah hollered above the clatter of rain. "You told them inside?"

"I didn't," Eric said guiltily. "He doesn't know."

Jonah looked at him strangely—accusingly, Eric thought—and then began to shamble away, muttering to himself.

"We need to get inside the museum," Eric called after him. "Can you show us?"

The clouds were suddenly lit up by a flash of lightning. A long, drawn-out roll of thunder spanned the sky.

"Listen, Ishmael," cried Jonah, turning back. "That's what the thunder said."

"Forget it, Eric," Chris said. "He's nuts."

"This way, this way," Jonah called out. "My home." He was moving towards the museum wall, looking back over his shoulder to see if they were following.

"This guy's utterly cracked," grumbled Chris.

"Come on," said Eric impatiently, brushing water out of his eyes.

Jonah walked aimlessly, letting his hand brush against the rough brick. He suddenly stooped, dropped to his knees and snatched up a long, glistening worm from the mud.

"Ah-ha!" he exclaimed. "Many more where that came from!"

Eric watched him with a sinking heart. Maybe Chris was right. This was turning into a wild goose chase. Jonah slipped the worm into one of his trouser pockets, pushed himself to his feet and stretched.

"X marks the spot," Jonah said triumphantly, pointing.

Hidden by a row of low shrubs was a metal grille in the museum wall. Jonah stooped again, swatted the spindly branches out of his way and yanked off the grille. Then, with surprising swiftness, he squeezed through the duct on all fours and scuttled out of sight.

"Follow the leader!" his voice rang out from inside.

"Ventilation duct," Eric said.

"It's kind of small," said Chris uncertainly.

"You'll fit," Eric told him. "Just suck in your chest."

"Easy for you to say," Chris retorted. "I don't disappear when I turn sideways."

Eric flushed, suddenly conscious of his hair plastered to his head, all his clothes clinging to his bony frame.

"You coming or not?" he asked hotly.

"Right behind you."

Eric crawled into the duct. It wasn't as narrow as he'd

thought. The metal floor dented loudly under the weight of his hands and knees. After only a few metres, the duct opened into a sizable junction where Jonah waited. There was enough light filtering in from the outside for Eric to see bottles, food tins, and bulging garbage bags strewn around the floor.

"Which way?" Eric asked, looking at all the ducts leading out of the junction.

Jonah rocked back and forth on his haunches a few times before knocking aside a garbage bag and revealing a grille in the floor. A blast of hot air hit Eric in the face. Its dank smell was the same as that in the cellars.

"No, to the museum," Eric reminded Jonah. "We want to get into the museum."

"Ah," said Jonah, and tilted his head up at a single metal grille in the ceiling.

"Thanks."

Eric pushed at it until it gave way. He tried to lift himself through, but his arms wouldn't do it. He swore under his breath. "Could you give me a boost?" he asked Chris without looking at him.

Chris cupped his hands and hefted Eric through the opening. It was dark. Eric walked carefully towards a line of light coming from underneath a door. His hand fumbled for a switch and the room was suddenly filled with light.

"It's just a storage room," he called back. "Come on up."

Chris hauled himself through without difficulty. "You sure he's going to be here?" he asked. "Won't he have left with everyone else?"

"No."

Eric opened the door and walked out into the immense machine workshop. It was deserted. Rain clattered against the high windows. All the equipment had been shut down.

"This place is utterly enormous," Chris whispered in awe.

Eric walked deeper into the room, at a loss. How would he ever find Alexander? Come on! he thought in frustration. You've been watching for me for ages. So where are you now?

A droning sound reached his ears, and he turned towards the freight elevator doors at the end of the workshop. Someone was coming up. The low rumble was getting louder. He motioned to Chris and they crouched behind a bank of machinery. Eric's heart raced. The elevator was taking forever to arrive.

Then there was a heavy thud, and the elevator doors split apart. Standing inside was Alexander, slumped against the wall, coughing.

Eric stepped out in relief.

"It's too late," Alexander said. "The live-forever machine is his now."

12

Another Step
to Hell

"He broke through the cellar wall," Alexander croaked. "Such a gaping hole! He must have had tools, blasting powder. And the ruin! Countless things scorched and shattered ..."

Alexander's voice trailed off as he caught sight of Chris. His eyes swept over Eric's companion suspiciously, lingering on the skull-shaped earring, the dyed slashes of colour across his ripped jeans.

"He's my friend," Eric explained nervously. He'd been in too much of a hurry to give any thought to how Alexander would react to Chris.

"I don't know you," Alexander said, dread flickering in his eyes. "I've not seen you before."

Chris's mouth moved as if he were about to reply, but he didn't say anything, only jammed his hands into his pockets and glanced helplessly at Eric. Eric suddenly felt sorry for Chris. He'd never seen his friend look so unsure of himself.

"I've told him everything," Eric said. "He's not going to—"

"How could you have done such a thing?" Alexander cried, turning on Eric. "I entrusted my secret to you. Him, I don't know. How can you be certain he is not in league with Coyle?"

Eric was chilled by the madness in Alexander's face.

"He's my friend," he said again, as forcefully as he could. "He's never even met Coyle!"

Alexander seemed to crumple, steadying himself against a worktable. "I hope he can be trusted." He cast a weary glance at Chris. "I hope he can hold the secrets." He pulled a handkerchief from a pocket and coughed violently into it.

Rain drummed fiercely against the windows. A brilliant flash of lightning froze them for a split second as if in a photograph.

"I remained behind as the museum was evacuated," said Alexander. "I knew the outburst of gas must have been Coyle's doing. I waited for him here, guarding the entrance to the cellars." He nodded at the freight elevator. "An hour passed, and then I felt the vibration through my feet, a rumble from deep within the earth. But by the time I reached the cellar, I was too late." He shook his head, incredulous. "Who would have thought that was to be his point of entrance?"

"We came to tell you," Eric said quietly. "He's been down on the main storm drain—I don't know for how long, but at least a week. He's got some kind of machinery down there. We heard it, something big."

He felt another sharp twist of guilt. Too late, he'd come too late.

Alexander nodded, mopping at his mouth with the handkerchief. "How did you get in?" he asked.

"Jonah showed—" Eric started again. "There's a guy who fishes through one of the storm drain grates behind the museum. He showed us how to get in through a tunnel, a ventilation duct, I guess. Jonah's a little crazy, but he knew about Coyle. He knew about the machinery Coyle's got down there."

"Some infernal engine, no doubt," said Alexander, "that will lay waste to all of this." He looked mournfully around the huge chamber. "It will all be consumed in flames. Now that he has the live-forever machine there is nothing to deter him."

"What will you do?" Eric asked.

Panic flickered in the ancient man's eyes, and a fit of coughing snapped his thin body over. "He will come for me soon," he said hoarsely. "My lunar cycle commenced last night. He can unmake me now. What alternative do I have but to fly, leave here at once? 'Shall Time's best jewel from Time's chest lie hid? / Or what strong hand can hold his swift foot back?' " His gaze seemed fixed on something invisible in the air before him. "So long has it been," he said in a croaking whisper. "But I recognize it now, one never truly forgets that dreaded face of death. How it glowers at me."

Eric shot a glance at Chris, who was staring at Alexander, his face frozen in amazement. What must he think? Eric wondered. Does he believe it now, or does he just think Alexander is insane? Eric looked from one to the other: Chris, so strong, so healthy-looking, skin tanned a light coffee brown, and Alexander, paler than Eric had ever seen him, his cheeks hollow, veins winding across his arms, his thin body caving in on itself.

"I must go at once," Alexander said.

"And just leave the museum?" cried Eric. He couldn't bear to think of it all destroyed: the dinosaur gallery, the Chinese tomb, the endless network of high-ceilinged halls. He should have taken the scroll.

"Don't you think it rends my heart also?" demanded Alexander. "But I am left with no other choice."

"Unmake him," Eric said.

"Sacrilege," Alexander whispered. "I won't be guilty of it. I would rather be pursued around the earth for an eternity than do such a thing."

It was insane. Coyle was going to kill Alexander, and he

wouldn't even act in his own defence. Eric gritted his teeth to keep from shouting out in anger and frustration.

"Forgive me, but there is no other—" Alexander stopped abruptly, and Eric could tell by his eyes that something had just occurred to him.

"What?"

"Coyle will not be able to read the scroll. It is written in the ancient languages, the dead languages from the documents I transcribed those long centuries ago. Coyle has forgotten them all."

Eric remembered the conversation in the medieval armoury, the panic in Coyle's voice when Alexander had spoken Latin. *Speak English.*

"The live-forever machine will be temporarily useless to him," Alexander went on, "though for how long, I cannot guess. He will translate it somehow."

"Computer," Chris said. He looked up from his sneakers. "A computer could do something like that. Remember—" he turned to Eric "—we saw him buy something in the computer store yesterday. He'd have to have a pretty powerful system, though, with a massive memory."

Alexander gazed at Chris, fascinated. "You understand this kind of machinery, do you, these computing devices? How long would the translation process take?"

Chris shrugged, unnerved by the intensity of Alexander's stare. "Depends how long the thing is, and how fast his system works. A while, anyway."

"So there is time," Alexander said softly, his eyes now on Eric. "Perhaps this computing device could be stopped, and the scroll recovered before Coyle translates it. The two of you ..."

Eric could see twin flames of hungry expectation dancing in the pupils of Alexander's extraordinary green eyes.

Alexander wanted the two of them to go down to the storm drains and steal back the live-forever machine.

"No way."

Chris's voice sounded a long way away. Eric's eyes were still locked with Alexander's. He felt the same tingle of partnership he'd experienced when the ancient librarian had pressed the locket into his hand that day in the corridor.

"Help me, Eric," said Alexander imploringly.

In his mind's eye, Eric saw Alexander walking through the cellar, touching things, speaking to them, overcome with memory. He cared only about his artifacts, his past. Just like Dad. They were both dinosaurs. But at least Alexander seemed to trust him, had told him his sixteen-hundred-year-old secret. And twice now Alexander had asked for Eric's help. Dad wouldn't do that, not ever. A tiny flame of anger bloomed within Eric. Maybe Dad was beyond help, didn't even want it. But at least Alexander was asking for help.

"Yes," he said. "All right."

"No!" Chris shook his head angrily. "No friggin' way! I'm not going down there, and you aren't either. This is stupid." He tossed his head in Alexander's direction. "Why doesn't *he* go down?"

"Think, think," Alexander said, with patronizing patience. "If Coyle has already completed the translation, he would unmake me instantly. In any event, what use would I be? It is you who has the expertise with these computing machines."

"He's right, Chris," Eric said.

"Crap," was his friend's reply. "All of this, crap."

"Shut up, Chris."

"Even your Dad would think this was utterly cracked. If you told him."

127

Eric glared at him. "Shut up, you jerk!"

Chris's face clouded over, his whole body went rigid, and for a second Eric thought Chris was going to hit him. He could feel the adrenalin pumping through his veins. He was going to get clobbered. He stared at Chris, not recognizing him, afraid, and then all at once the hatred evaporated, leaving only a sick lump in his stomach.

"Are you coming?" he asked, looking away.

"No!" Chris shouted. "This isn't like going down to see the furnace room, Eric. This isn't like going down a manhole. This is crazy and dangerous."

Alexander watched them in silence, his fingers nervously tracing the outline of his pale mouth.

"I can't go alone, Chris. I don't know anything about computers."

Chris just looked at the rain sheeting down the windows.

"Come on," said Eric, forcing a smile. "You're the muscle, remember? You can't let a skinny geek like me go down there alone. If it's too dangerous, we'll come back."

"Eric—"

"It's almost the end of the summer. You won't ever have to talk to me again afterwards." That was what Chris really wanted anyway, Eric thought ruefully. To go back to school and hang around with all his friends while Eric just faded away. "Last adventure of the summer," he said.

"Don't even know if I believe any of this," Chris grumbled, scratching at his blond hair. "How would we get down to the storm drain? We can't go through the cellar; he's probably watching there. Maybe I could run off a hard copy of Mom's blueprints—"

"Jonah can show us the way," said Eric. "He's been down there."

"You sure?"

"He knew about Coyle before any of us," Eric reminded him. "He must have gone there himself. He knew what Coyle looked like. He must have seen the machinery. That shaft he showed us in his tunnel—it must lead down to the drains."

"I don't know, Eric; I think we should get the blueprints."

The overhead lights in the workshop flickered, then flared. The bulbs exploded. Eric protected his face against the shower of glass.

"Electricity's gone," he said, carefully shaking splinters of glass out of his hair and clothing.

"It's starting," Alexander said, so softly his words were barely audible.

"He must be plugging into the city's wiring," murmured Chris.

"There's no time for the blueprints," Eric said. "We've got to go."

"Wait a second—just like this?" cried Chris, holding out his empty hands.

"What would you suggest?" Alexander asked mockingly.

Chris flushed. "I don't know. But something." His eyes flicked across the workbench. "Anything. *That.*"

Alexander picked up the wood chisel and examined the long, sharp edge. "You think this would serve you well, do you? You can imagine yourself heroically driving this into Coyle's immortal neck?" He slapped his hand palm down on the table, raised the chisel and drove it into his flesh, so forcefully that Eric could hear the metal blade bite into the wood of the workbench beneath.

"Shit!" Chris gasped, his eyes wide with shock.

Eric watched, sickened, as Alexander withdrew the chisel. There was very little blood, only a long red gash in the middle of his hand that already seemed to be closing

129

over, healing, until soon there was only a strip of shiny pink scar tissue.

"That is what it is to be immortal," Alexander said, throwing the chisel back onto the table.

"This is utterly crazy," Chris said, unconsciously rubbing the palm of his left hand. "This is so damn crazy."

"Surprise will be your weapon," Alexander said, beginning to cough again. In horror, Eric watched as a bloody stain appeared on the handkerchief. It was far worse than the fleeting gash the chisel had made—this was blood coming from deep inside.

"Yes," Alexander said huskily, catching Eric's eye. "I've been sick for more than sixteen hundred years now, since before I made myself immortal. For whatever disability or disease you have when you make yourself, you carry with you for eternity. It's the wasting illness, the consumption. It won't kill me, but neither will it leave me."

Eric swallowed. A tremor of fear moved through his body. Chris is right, a part of him was saying; this is crazy and dangerous. He gritted his teeth, tightened his whole body to stop the trembling inside. He had to try to save museum. It was the only thing left. The unchanging things he'd looked at his entire life, the dates. Everything else was falling apart. His mother, his father. Think of the dates. Battle of Waterloo, 1815. Sinking of the Titanic, 1912. There, that was better. The dates never changed.

He looked at Chris. "We should go find Jonah," he said.

They found him in the ventilation duct, sitting on a stack of sodden newspapers, making a knot in the rung of a rope ladder. A steady stream of water from outside licked around his garbage bags. Eric could hear the rain, amplified through the metal tunnel, knocking leaves off trees, battering the ground.

Jonah finished tying his knot and then looked up. He didn't seem at all surprised to see them, Eric thought. With a crooked grin that showed a mouthful of discoloured teeth, Jonah pointed down to the grille in the floor. The rain water swirled through the steel mesh into darkness. Eric couldn't hear it hit bottom.

"Can you take us down?" he asked. "Show us where he is—the machinery, the noise?" He had no idea how he should talk to the half-crazed Jonah. Leave out words longer than five letters? Make hand signals?

Jonah nodded thoughtfully, as if weighing a very small child's ridiculous request. "All right, Ishmael," he said. "All right, Odysseus; all right, Aeneas; all right, Marlowe."

Chris wrinkled his face at the smell of the man's breath.

Jonah prised off the metal covering with long, dirty fingernails, and deftly tied one end of his rope ladder to a pair of metal loops. He tested the knot, then tossed over the rest of the ladder.

"Down and down and down," he sang as he swung himself into the shaft. "Twenty thousand leagues under the sea!"

Eric didn't give himself any time to get scared. As soon as Jonah's head dipped out of sight, he grabbed hold of the ladder and carefully lowered himself through the opening. He could feel the rungs go taut, then slack, then taut again as Jonah descended with chimpanzee ease. Eric's arms trembled, and he could feel the tendons on the inside of his elbow standing out like steel cable. Fear or weakness? Both, he decided with disgust.

A warm drizzle of rain water fell over him, dampening his hair and clothing, trickling down his sleeves and collar onto his bare skin. He looked up and saw Chris climbing down above him, silhouetted against the square of light from the opening.

"Careful!" he called out. "You nearly stepped on my fingers." His voice sounded hollow and metallic, bouncing against the metal walls.

A humid stench wafted up in sickening waves. The ladder swayed and stretched. With every fearful step Eric took, it got darker, until he could barely see his own hands clamped around the rungs. He heard a distant rumble through the shaft. The subway. Reflexively, he thought of his father. Had Dad really come down here once, to the very bottom? He caught himself wishing, for just a second, that his father were with them now, guiding them through the darkness. He forced the thought out of his mind, concentrated on the ladder.

His foot prodded empty air. His hands instinctively tightened like vises around the rope. Bottomless pit. Dream free-fall. He couldn't stop the panicked cry that escaped his throat.

"What's wrong?" came Chris's startled voice.

Before Eric could answer, he felt Jonah's malodorous breath against his face and a hand closed around his thin arm, urging him gently off the ladder. He stepped to the floor, his heart still clattering.

"It's all right," he said to Chris. "It's just the ladder; it ends here. You can step down."

They were in a tunnel with a low ceiling—no higher than six feet, he guessed. Wet ran down the concrete walls, glistening darkly between the pipes and cables, dripping over rusted valves and wheels.

"It stinks down here," Chris said.

"It's the gas," Eric told him, "mixed with this stale air."

132

Jonah tapped his knuckles against one of the pipes. It gave off a hollow ring. He cocked his head to one side thoughtfully and flicked another pipe. A slightly higher tone rang out. He struck a third pipe and noted its sound. Then he started slapping at all the pipes at once, as if he were playing some bizarre musical instrument, laughing gleefully.

"Oh, geez," Chris groaned. "An utter nightmare."

Jonah stopped abruptly, and started along the tunnel. "The village," he said. "Family and friends."

Eric hurried after the muttering man. What was Jonah talking about now? Mice darted across the floor, disappearing through crevices in the stone, and he saw a rat perched on a cable, gnawing through the insulation. At least Eric couldn't smell the dank stench anymore. He felt slightly unreal, cut off from the world, as he had in the cellar.

"Why isn't Alexander down here with us?" Chris violently knocked a low-hanging cable out of their way. "He's using us."

"He can't risk it," Eric reminded Chris. "He told us why." But he knew Chris was right. Alexander cared only about getting the scroll back. He'd lived too long to care about people; Gabriella della Signatura had been his only mistake. How could loving someone be a mistake? Eric shuddered in the damp heat. Don't think about it, he chided himself. Battle of Hastings, 1066. Coronation of Charlemagne, 800.

"What if something happens to us?" Chris said, coming to a stop. "No one knows we're down here. And he's not going to tell anyone."

"You're right," said Eric impatiently. Jonah was ambling on ahead, getting swallowed up in the darkness. "He is using us. He doesn't care what happens to us as long as we stop Coyle from translating the scroll."

"Then why are we doing this?" Chris demanded.

"If we get the scroll back, the museum's safe," Eric told him. "Coyle wouldn't risk burning it down if the live-forever machine were still inside."

That was only part of it, though. Eric didn't want to see Alexander destroyed, even if he was crazy and ruthless. At least he believed in something. He believed in the objects, the past, the dates. Hardly anyone cared anymore. All people wanted was shopping malls and TV disasters. Be careful, he told himself, you're beginning to think like Alexander. And Dad.

"Come on," he said to Chris. "We've got to catch up."

Jonah was waiting for them up ahead, doing chin-ups on a pipe. He did five more, then dropped down and scurried away, mumbling about the rain.

At last the tunnel opened into a large chamber. Dark shapes shifted in the gloom. Eric's skin crawled. There were other people here, sprawled on tattered blankets or inflatable air mattresses, huddled in small groups, eating and drinking out of dented tin cans, talking quietly. A few people read tattered paperbacks in the flickering candle-light. Eric recognized the man who preached the wrath of God on the street corner outside the farm house. And the woman digging her fork into a tin can: she was the one who spent whole days shaking her fist at billboards, shouting until spittle flew from her mouth. In the corner was the street vendor who arrived at the museum every day with a strange three-wheeled trolley that he rode like a bicycle. And over there, the young man who wandered through the city streets with his imaginary dog.

The vagrants were noticing them now, twisting around for a better look. As Jonah left his side and went towards them, Eric wanted to plead, Don't leave us standing alone like this. It was stupid; what did he expect, anyway? For crazy Jonah to protect him from all the other crazy people? For a moment, he wanted to run from this subterranean madhouse before something terrible happened.

"I think this is the part where we get robbed, tied up, and left in the dark for the rats," Chris whispered.

Jonah was talking to the vagrants in turn, touching someone's shoulder, whispering in someone's ear. Eric's heart contracted as the billboard lady shuffled towards him, stooped under the weight of layers of clothing and a parka. How can she stand it in this heat? he wondered. She peered into his face and then grabbed his wrist. Eric flinched, ready to break free, but she was only shaking his hand as if congratulating him, muttering something inaudible.

"This place is nuts," Chris said when she'd tramped away. "How'd they all get down here?"

"Like we did, I guess—storm drain grates, manholes."

Eric noticed that a few of the vagrants were sitting on the gutted casings of televisions. In one corner, a rusted bicycle frame had been stood upside down and turned into a kind of clothes rack. An ironing board was being used as a shelf for tattered paperbacks, chipped crockery, bent knives and forks. An ancient record player had somehow been converted into a hotplate.

"Where did they get all this stuff?" he mumbled, gazing around the room.

Piled against the far wall of the chamber was a huge junk heap. He walked closer. His eyes picked out a child's mitten, a three-legged coffee table, a clock with no arms, a woman's purse, a doll's head, a ragged copy of *Moby Dick*, a pair of glasses, a school textbook, a scarf.

"What is all this crap?" Chris said disdainfully.

They must have been collecting it for years, Eric thought

in amazement. All these bits of people's lives, forgotten in bus shelters and subway stations, thrown out in back alleys and garbage dumpsters.

He couldn't help thinking of Alexander's cellars, the heaps of beautiful old things. What was the use of them when they were hidden away? No one would ever get to see them, no one would ever touch them except Alexander. At least the vagrants had found something useful to do with their old things.

Jonah was picking through the heap, bending closer to look, slipping things into his pockets.

"Hey, take a look at this," Chris said, edging forward and pulling at something from the vast pile. "Now we're talking!"

It was an old-fashioned machine gun, right out of a 1930s gangster film.

"Wonder if it—?" Chris squeezed the trigger. Nothing happened. He shook the gun violently and tried again. "Busted. Well, this is definitely coming with me."

"Why? It's not going to do you any good—it wouldn't help even if it did work," Eric told him irritably.

Chris shrugged. "Makes me feel better." He grabbed an old tablecloth from the junk heap and ripped off a broad swath for a shoulder strap.

"We have to go," Eric called out to Jonah, afraid that he'd forgotten them. "How do we get down to the storm drain?"

Jonah shuffled back towards them, his cupped hands filled with garbage.

"Um, thanks," Eric said, holding out his own hands as Jonah let the debris fall into them. He jammed it hurriedly into his pocket. Jonah then cornered Chris, who looked dubiously at the dusty gift cascading into his hands. As soon as Jonah's back was turned, Chris let it all drop to the floor.

"The storm drains?" Eric said again hopefully.

Without a word, Jonah headed towards a corridor leading out of the chamber.

He'd lost all sense of time.

It could have been twenty minutes or two hours; Eric didn't know anymore. Jonah had led them through a maze of low corridors, down flights of crumbling steps, singing scraps of songs Eric had never heard, laughing just to hear his own voice echoing back at him.

The sound of water had been getting steadily louder. Eric could hear its hollow metallic rush as it tumbled through hidden grates, bubbled through unseen pipes. He watched it seeping down the tunnel walls, dripping from the ceiling and pooling underfoot.

Jonah stopped and pushed a piece of corrugated metal away from the wall, revealing a skeletal metal stairway that twisted downwards. The sound of rushing water rose up to them like a geyser.

"Down here?" Eric asked wearily.

Jonah turned and started back the way he'd come.

"How do we know where to find him?"

"Down, down, down," Jonah said, not looking back.

"Hey!" Chris yelled. "Come back!" But Jonah had been swallowed up in darkness. "That's just great!"

"Forget it," Eric said. "This must go down to the drain. Listen to the water."

He took the first step, then another. After a moment he could hear Chris coming down behind him. Sweat trickled over his eyebrows, burning his face. The sound of water was all around them now, churning and rolling, booming like the sea.

13

Tar Machine
Heart

"Underground river," Eric breathed.

He shielded his eyes against the warm spray thrown off by the torrent churning through the storm drain. It ran down the centre of an immense concrete cavern, with walls that towered up overhead into darkness. Eric could make out distant pinpricks of glittering light—lamps or vent openings to the outside, he guessed. Somewhere up there was the metal platform he and Chris had stood on. They were a long way down.

Pipes were everywhere, clamped against the walls, thrusting up from the cement floor, spanning the cavern. Some fed directly into the storm drain, spewing out water from grates across the flooded city. Cables sagged from the walls or twined around the pipes, throbbing with electricity.

Clank! Clank, clank, clank!

The sound of machinery hammered through the hot air. Eric peered into the twilight murk, trying to find the source. A moment later, a dusting of sulphurous soot stung his eyes and nose.

"He must have some wicked machinery to be spewing out crap like that." Chris spit to clear his mouth.

Was it some kind of bomb, Eric wondered, as Alexander thought? He remembered Jonah's babble over the storm drain grate: fire and brimstone. He imagined huge metallic limbs grinding against one another, sparks, electric eyes that glimmered in the darkness. What could Coyle have built down here?

"Come on," he said to Chris, and they headed along the shore of the storm drain, sticking close to the cover of the pipes and cables. The water churned thunderously through the cavern. It must be raining like the end of the world up there, Eric thought.

"Look over there," Chris said. "What is that?" He was pointing to the far side of the cavern. High up on the wall, above a network of sagging catwalks, were two rows of large spoked wheels.

"Maybe valves to control the water," Eric guessed, looking at the pipes and cables knotted around the wheels. He could make out old-fashioned levers and lighted gauges with needles clicking from side to side. Giant electric heart, he thought—the humming wires nerves, the zigzagging pipes veins, the storm drain an artery, pumping the water through the city.

"They look pretty ancient," Chris said, shaking his head. His machine gun swung against a pipe, making a hollow clang.

Eric looked at it disapprovingly. "Why don't you get rid of that thing?"

"I only wish it worked," said Chris.

"It's stupid," Eric snapped. "It's just going to get in the way. Get rid of it."

Chris's powerful shoulders hunched slightly, his arms tightened by his sides, and he turned slowly to face Eric. "Everything I do is stupid, isn't it? You want to hear stupid? Being here! This is the stupidest thing I can think of, so don't tell me *I'm* stupid."

"You know why we came down here!" Eric shouted back. "It's not stupid! We're trying to save the museum.

139

How many times do I have to explain before it gets through your thick head?"

"Should have listened to my friends," Chris said. "They were right, you know. Know what they say about you?"

"I have a pretty good idea, but go ahead." His heart was throbbing like a gyroscope. This was it, he thought; this was how it would end, with a big fight, right here on the storm drain.

"They're always saying what a loser you are. They're right, you're a total wimp loser."

"At least I'm not the one whining every step of the way like some blond Neanderthal!"

Something dark and sleek brushed past Chris's head and swooped up into the cavern.

"What the hell was that?" Chris yelled, clutching his face.

Eric could make out a cluster of the dark shapes, darting erratically through the air.

"Bats," he whispered.

They were wheeling, swooping back. There was something terrifying about them, even the thought of them, flying around your face, their leathery skin grazing you. Here they come. Eric threw his arm up over his face and turned his back. They whistled by, and he could feel the tips of their wings brush against his hair. Beside him, Chris shouted and cursed.

Then they were gone.

Chris had fallen to his knees with both arms covering his head.

"It's all right, they're gone," Eric told him shakily.

Chris's breathing was fast and shallow, and his eyes were widened in panic.

"You all right?" Eric asked, slumping down beside him. "They're gone. Just bats. They're harmless."

"I can't breathe." Chris's eyes darted frantically around the cavern and Eric was afraid he was about to bolt and run. "Can't breathe!"

"Yes, you can," Eric said, trying not to let his own fear show. "You're just scared. Take a deep breath; go ahead."

Chris shook his head desperately.

"I'm gonna die!"

"No, you're not. Come on, Chris. You're all right. You're all right." He didn't know what else to say, so he kept repeating the same three words over and over until Chris's breathing slowed and his eyes lost their terrified gleam.

"I thought I was going to die," Chris finally said. "That was utterly scary." He looked quickly up at Eric, embarrassed. "That's never happened to me before."

Eric just shrugged—it didn't matter. He never thought he'd see something like this: sports superstar Chris, so afraid he couldn't take a deep breath. But, it didn't give him even a glimmer of mean satisfaction. He suddenly felt frightened himself. What *were* they doing down here?

Trying to save Alexander, he told himself as calmly as he could. Trying to save the museum, the Chinese tomb, the dinosaur gallery. But somehow the memories of those visits with his father weren't the same anymore. Eric's jaw tightened. The two of them had probably wound up there just so Dad could brood over Mom, think about her while looking at all the old things.

"He's crazy," Eric said, choking out the words. "Dad's such a freak."

Chris was looking at him in alarm.

"What d'you mean?" he stammered. "He's okay."

Eric shook his head. "No, he's not. He's some kind of freak, just the way everyone thinks. Remember I told you my Mom died in an accident? That's a lie. He lied to me.

141

She jumped in front of a train—that's how she really died. He never told me until a couple days ago."

There, he'd said it. He felt numb.

"It's been thirteen years and he still can't forget her. He *enjoys* being unhappy. He's crazy."

"Must be a hard thing to forget," Chris mumbled, as if he didn't know what else to say.

"Thirteen years!" Eric exclaimed. "And why are you sticking up for him? He hates you; he thinks you're an idiot!"

He was sorry the moment he saw Chris's face.

Chris shrugged. "So do you," he said coldly.

"What? That's not true!"

"Every chance you get, reminding me how stupid I am!"

Eric felt a sick swirling in his guts. It was true.

"Why do you think I'm doing this, anyway?" Chris stormed. "So you won't think I'm a moron. That's the only reason—so maybe you'll think I'm not just some sports dork with no brain!"

Eric stared at his knees; he couldn't look at Chris. He'd never stopped feeling like a skinny geek around Chris—so he put Chris down to get even. He felt another wave of queasiness crash over him.

"Let's go back," he said.

He felt empty and alone. It was pointless. Even if they did get the scroll and stop Coyle, things wouldn't be any different. His father would still think about Mom and never love him as much. And he'd keep on getting hurt. And Chris would still hate him. Nothing would change.

"No way!" Chris said, scrambling to his feet. He still sounded angry. "No friggin' way am I going back now! We got all the way down here. And besides, I don't want to give up my chance at being a big hero. You never know, I might even get on Split Second News!" He smiled a little, as if it was a joke. "You don't want to go back, either."

It was true. Eric nodded wearily. Had to try to save the museum, save the dates. They were the only things you could rely on. Invention of photography, 1827. Michelangelo's *David*, 1501. He pushed himself up from the damp concrete and they started walking again.

Up ahead, a blue glow shimmered along the shore of the storm drain—pale at first, suddenly brightening, then fading again.

"Look," said Eric, nodding his head in the direction of the gleam. In the distance was a huge, conical silhouette at the edge of the storm drain, backlit by the blue flicker. Chris, one hand steadying his gun, led the way deeper into the tangle of cables and pipes against the wall; Eric followed behind him.

"What *is* that?" Eric whispered as they drew closer.

It was unlike any machine he'd ever seen, old and new at the same time. It was shaped like the spire of a Gothic cathedral. It bristled with copper wires and electronic components, multicoloured bundles of cable, tiny video screens, panels of twinkling lights, long levers and pistons like something from the undercarriage of a locomotive. Turning cog-wheels meshed like the insides of an old-fashioned clock. A spiral of steaming tubing surrounded the base of the machine, funnelling water in from pipes along the storm drain.

As Eric and Chris watched, one of the contraption's massive levers began to turn slowly—one, two, three clanking, deafening revolutions, and then a huge burst of black smoke exploded from its innards into the cavern.

"I don't know," Chris was shaking his head in amazement. "I don't know what that is."

Blue light flickered over the machine, over the water's tumultuous surface. Eric moved cautiously forward for a better look, ducking around the cavern's steel undergrowth. He shoved a cable out of his way.

About twenty metres beyond the machine tower sat a pyramid of fifteen televisions flashing out commercials, soap operas, game shows, Split Second News spots, a video shopping program. In front of the TV pyramid, at a long table covered with electronic equipment, stood Coyle, staring intently into a glowing computer monitor. Occasionally, without looking away, he would type something onto the keyboard, adjust a switch. He stood very still and straight, his whole body bathed in the light of the screen. Bars of green flickered across his chest, red symbols danced over his face. Then the colours changed, sweeping over him in broad swaths so that he seemed to be made of light, a projection from the screen itself.

Beyond the television pyramid, Eric could see rubble and metal debris strewn across the floor, and a dark, jagged opening blasted in the cavern wall. Right into the cellar. Tools were spread out nearby—a jackhammer, picks and crowbars, a sledgehammer. Must have had dynamite, too, to make a hole that big.

"Amazing." Chris's eyes were darting over the machinery assembled on Coyle's table.

"Explain all this to me," said Eric, his voice all but drowned out by the roar of water. "What's that?" He pointed to a large machine that looked like a photocopier. A slab of light moved rhythmically back and forth across the glass surface.

"Optical scanner," Chris told him. "It's bigger than any I've ever seen, too. Must be really precise. Look, he's got the scroll feeding through it. The scanner reads it—all the letters, or whatever it's written in—and shoots it all back into the computer."

"Where it gets translated, right? Is that the computer there, the screen he's watching?"

"Part of it, anyway," Chris answered, squinting. "There's got to be more than that, though. He's got a couple of external drives, maybe some decent hard memory inside ..." He shook his head, confused. "Not enough. For what he's doing, there's no way it's enough." His face went blank for a second. "Geez," he muttered.

"What?"

Chris nodded at the huge tower of machinery on the shore of the storm drain.

"*That's* the memory."

"That?"

"The computer feeds right into it. Look, follow the patch cables. It must have eight or ten stacks. That's big, Eric, really big. Enough to hold, I don't know, an entire library— more, even." There was admiration in his voice. "It all makes perfect sense. Unlimited power supply from the electrical grid, lots of water to cool the thing. Perfect. I can't believe he built this thing himself. He must be some kind of genius."

The optical scanner emitted a rapid series of beeps, and the bar of light slowly faded out. Coyle lifted the shield and pulled out a long scroll of parchment. The live-forever machine.

"Is that it?" Eric asked, worried. "Is it finished?"

"The scanning is, yeah. Everything's gone into the computer, but it can't all be translated yet."

Coyle quickly rolled up the scroll and slipped it back into the white canister. He looked back at the monitor, touched the keyboard and then walked away from the table, towards the hole leading to the museum cellar. He disappeared through the gap.

"We've got to grab the scroll," Eric said.

"Not that simple," Chris told him. "It's in there now, too, remember?" He jabbed a finger in the direction of the memory tower.

"Can we shut it off?"

Chris snorted. "Even if we could, it wouldn't help. A memory like that would still hold onto everything. It's like a vault." His eyes moved slowly up and down the machine. "Yeah, it must be smart as anything."

"Well, maybe you could figure something out if you'd stop gazing at it so lovingly!"

"It's an incredible piece of machinery, that's all!"

"Sorry."

"Yeah, well." He was still looking at the machine. Its huge levers were turning again; clank, clank, clank, and then the billowing smog. "A power surge might do it," Chris said.

"Would that erase the memory?"

"Maybe, but there's no way we could pull it off. You'd need to send a lot of extra voltage through the power lines." Eric followed his gaze to the machine's base, encircled by corrugated tubing. It glistened darkly, wet with moisture, pulsing slightly from the water pressure.

"The water," Chris said. "Cut it off."

Eric nodded slowly. "It'll overheat."

"Yeah. And something that big, when it overheats, it'll probably melt the memory boards. Don't know how we'd do it, though."

Eric's eyes flicked back to the hole in the cavern wall. Coyle had reappeared, carrying several small oil paintings under one arm, and a clay statuette under the other. He set the artifacts down by the table in front of the televisions and proceeded to rip the paintings apart with his bare hands, snapping the wooden frames across his leg, clawing the canvas into rags. Then he hefted the statuette, looked at it contemptuously for a moment, and hurled it against the wall, where it exploded into dust.

Anger smouldered inside Eric. This was a hundred times worse than what he'd seen in the medieval armoury. Coyle's twisted face, the sound of splintering wood, ripping canvas, disintegrating stone—it was completely insane.

He looked back at the machine, steaming by the storm drain, its electronic innards translating languages thousands of years old. Chris was right, they had been idiots to come down here empty-handed. What was wrong with them!

He pressed his palms against his exhausted legs and felt the bulge of Jonah's junk in his pocket. He reached in, grabbed it. Chris craned his neck to look. Eric blew away the clots of dust and shredded paper and was surprised at how little there really was. In his cupped hands he held a small metal paperweight and a nail.

He drove the nail in with the flat of the paperweight. Three fast blows and the sharp tip pierced the rubber tubing. He yanked back the nail and a narrow jet of warm water spurted out.

"One," he whispered to Chris.

It hadn't been difficult to reach the memory tower. Coyle's back was almost fully turned to them, and the cables and pipes had hidden them as they darted in, crouched low. Eric was amazed at the thing's size—it was much taller than it had looked from the distance, maybe four metres high. Oil lines glistened like snakes across its dark surface. Cogwheels meshed with a whisper. Eric could feel the heat from its metal innards. A black smell poisoned the air, thick as tar. His skin tingled; the hairs on his forearms stood on end.

"Electric charge," said Chris, watching the hairs on his own arms. "This thing really puts out."

Spray from the torrent surging through the storm drain hung in the hot air. Eric blinked to clear his eyes. He moved the nail over and hammered it in farther along the corrugated tubing. Another stream shot out, drenching his shirt. He smiled, repositioned the nail and drove it home again. The roar of water drowned out his hammer strikes.

Chris peered cautiously around the base of the machine.

"Where is he?" Eric asked.

"Still there at the monitor."

"How many holes do we need?"

"A lot. It'll take a while to overheat. It's not going to happen right away."

Eric didn't say anything. He kept on hammering the nail through the piping. His arm fell into a robotic rhythm; his mind emptied itself. All he was aware of was the water, pooling around his knees, arching through the air. He hardly noticed that the fingers of his left hand were bleeding, battered again and again between the paperweight and head of the nail.

"Listen, listen," Chris was saying.

"What?" Eric felt as if he'd been jolted out of a daydream.

"It's starting."

The machine's buzz had changed pitch slightly, the sound of meshing gears a little more laboured now. Eric brushed a hand across his forehead, sweeping away sweat.

"It's getting hotter, too," he said. "Will he notice?"

"Might. Depends if he gets a warning on the monitor." He looked around the machine again. "Hang on. I think he's going back to the cellar."

148

Eric leaned over and watched as Coyle disappeared through the hole in the cavern wall. His eyes flicked back to the long table where the white canister lay, gleaming in the wash of television light.

"How much longer before it overheats?" he asked Chris urgently.

Chris shook his head. "No idea."

"I'm going to go grab the scroll." He pressed the nail and paperweight into Chris's hand. "Keep hammering."

Crouched low, he scuttled out from behind the memory tower and along the storm drain. He hardly felt attached to his own body; he was just a set of eyes scanning the cavern as his legs moved him closer to the television pyramid. Still no sign of Coyle. Quick. Quick. He darted over to the long table. The noise from the televisions swirled around him like a dust tornado.

"... and would you believe the swimming pool alone cost over three million ..."

"... streets flooded ..."

"... I'll take Rock Stars for a hundred ..."

"... luxury as you've never ..."

"... disaster struck again ..."

"... won a brand new ..."

"... latest in high fashion ..."

"... blockbuster smash ..."

"... hundred victims ..."

Eric grabbed the white canister.

"... I can see you ..."

Eric felt his skin prickle with terror. He slowly looked up at the array of flashing screens. On the television at the top of the pyramid was Coyle's face, eyes looking straight into his own.

"Gotcha," Coyle said, and the screen went black.

Eric whirled, a cry bottled in his throat, his fingers tightening convulsively around the canister. Coyle had emerged from the hole in the cavern wall, a rifle readied at his shoulder. In his paralyzed panic, Eric almost laughed: everyone wanted a gun, he thought. But this one looked real.

"Drop it," Coyle called out, striding towards him. "Hands in the air where I can see them. Freeze. Don't try to run for it or I'll blow your head off." Coyle must have gotten his lines from a TV cop show, Eric thought. "You know what this is?" Coyle went on, giving the rifle a little shake. "It's a lightning gun. Ever seen one? It shoots out a stream of negative ions, then builds up a positive charge. The spark leaps. Lightning. Hurts more than bullets."

At least with Alexander there had been clues of his age—his speech, his musty smell, his emaciated body, his cough. With Coyle there was nothing. Except, Eric now noticed, the eyes: they were an unreal neon blue.

"Alexander sent you," said Coyle, darting glances around the cavern. "Right?"

Eric nodded. What other reason could he give for being down here, hundreds of metres below the city?

"Where is he?"

There was alarm in Coyle's eyes. Maybe Alexander was right, Eric thought; he hadn't expected anyone to find his hiding place so easily.

"He's going to unmake you." He took the chance and blurted it out, watching Coyle's face for a reaction. The immortal's eyes darkened to the colour of deep sea water and a smile tugged at the corners of his mouth.

"Old Alexander's told you a lot, hasn't he?"

Eric said nothing.

"You're wrong, you know. He won't unmake me. He's afraid to do it. He's had his chances, hundreds of them."

Coyle raised his eyebrows. "Where is he now? Is he here?" When Eric didn't answer, Coyle tapped the hot muzzle of the gun against his chin. "Is he with you?"

"No."

"He sent you to do his dirty work, didn't he? To steal my scroll?" He studied Eric carefully for a moment. "But I suppose he said it was his. We worked on it together, didn't he tell you? It's mine as much as his."

"He said you were his research assistant. You stole his working notes."

Coyle's pupils contracted like dark whirlpools. For a moment, it seemed he was trying to remember something, but quickly gave up. "Well, that's wrong," he said harshly. "He lies a lot, you know. You can't trust him. We were partners. But when we finished, he wanted all the credit for himself. We weren't even going to try to use it. But he broke his promise, and tried to hide it from me."

Eric's stomach felt queasy. Had Coyle really forgotten everything, as Alexander had said? Was he just making this up? He said it with such conviction.

"He was the first to make himself," Coyle said again. "He didn't tell you that, did he? That cough of his? It's TB. Tuberculosis. He was sick. He knew he'd die soon if he didn't make himself immortal."

Eric thought of the blood on the handkerchief. The wasting illness, Alexander had said. It made sense. Anyone would do something drastic if they knew they were going to die otherwise. Was that all it was? Coyle's version made sense, too! How would he ever know who was telling the truth?

He let his eyes flick to the computer tower. How much longer before it overheated?

"And there was another thing," Coyle said softly. "Greed.

Did he show you his private hoard in the cellar? He just keeps it all to himself, doesn't he?" Coyle tapped the side of his skull. "He's crazy. That stuff was just falling apart."

Eric was beginning to feel lightheaded. He thought of Alexander, walking through his cellar, speaking Latin to his treasures—the things he was letting tarnish and rot in the damp.

"At least he didn't smash them," Eric said hoarsely. He had to talk, to convince himself that Alexander wasn't mad. "I saw what you did to those things."

Coyle's smooth face tightened. "They were old and ugly and broken," he said in a dangerously soft voice. "There's no *point* to them anymore. Alexander doesn't see that. He's crazy. What else has he told you, what other lies?"

"Everything about you," Eric said contemptuously.

"Really?" There was a look of amusement on Coyle's face. But the smile contracted into a snarl. "Did he tell you about this?" With his free hand he reached for his T-shirt hem and yanked it up. A broad, jagged line of scar tissue ran from his navel to his breastbone.

Eric felt his stomach rise.

"He didn't tell you about that?" Coyle said, letting his shirt drop again. "He was waiting for me in the dark. He slammed me through with a spear. I was pinned to the wall like a bug. It didn't kill me, but the pain! He wanted to see me suffer, kept twisting the blade in my guts. Then he locked me in a cell."

The Louvre. Alexander had trapped Coyle, and sealed him in an underground vault. But he hadn't said anything about stabbing him. That scar. Eric tried to swallow, but his throat was too dry and he thought he might choke. Could Alexander really have done that?

"You were trying to steal the scroll," Eric said, locking his

152

eyes on his sneakers. "You wanted to unmake him. He was just trying to protect himself—the museums, too."

"No," Coyle said. "He's dangerous. He's got to be unmade. Don't you see that? He's lost his grip." His voice was like a whisper in Eric's ear now. "How can you believe anything he says? He sends you down here alone to steal back the scroll, to do his dirty work! Why didn't he come himself? Didn't he tell you the danger? He's a coward. He's using you."

Eric had known as much all along. But he'd still decided to come down and try to stop Coyle from translating the live-forever machine. Why? He forced himself to go over the reasons. For the museum. For the old things. Discovery of King Tut's tomb, 1922. War of the Roses, 1450. And for the first time he wondered if he was doing it for his father, too. Would Dad be proud of him, wanting to save all the things he talked about his whole life? Would doing this change anything between them?

"The live-forever machine," Coyle said, poking at the white canister with his rifle. "Did Alexander tell you that's what he called it? He doesn't know what a machine is! This is just crumbling paper. I could tear it to pieces! A machine is metal guts, it's steel cable, it's silicon chips, it's heat and smoke!" He nodded in the direction of the memory tower. "That," he said, his neon blue eyes gleaming, "is the true live-forever machine."

Eric looked at the technical manuals stacked on the table—thick coil-bound volumes on electrical engineering, computer languages, artificial intelligence—sheaves of paper covered with columns of numbers and complex formulae. Coyle had built the thing himself.

Some kind of genius—wasn't that what Chris had said?

"Poor Alexander," Coyle said patronizingly. "Spending all

his time slinking around rotting old things! They're useless to us now; their time is over and done with! How can we plunge ahead into our glorious future if we're always looking back over our shoulders, being pulled back by the dreary, dead past. Alexander hates the present and fears the future. The future! Bigger, faster, better. The glorious future soars forward at a million kilometres a second. The past stands still, frozen. We must press ahead! Forget everything. Destroy it all!"

Coyle shouted out his words with the ferocity of a fanatic, sweeping his arms back and forth, waving the lightning-maker. Maybe he was right, Eric suddenly thought. What use was the past? Look at Alexander, coughing up sixteen-hundred-year-old blood, trying to remember everything, treasure everything—except people. He didn't know what being alive was. And you, Dad, he thought: wouldn't it be better if you could stop thinking about her, dying over and over again in your mind. Just forget her.

"Do you see it?" Coyle cried out. "The world is new and improved every day. There are machines all around us, wonderful, beautiful machines that power cars and jets, build buildings, open doors, send images across the world! Forget about the past! Let me tell you about optical fibres, genetic engineering, super aluminum and space probes! I'm talking about androids and artificial intelligence, machines that can talk, shop and walk the dog. I can see cities a thousand storeys high. I can see vehicles faster and sleeker. I can see the future bigger and brighter!"

Perspiration beaded his forehead. Spit was collecting in a white rim at the corners of his mouth. Television light played over his face.

"We have to start right away! Right now!" Coyle roared. "The glorious future awaits us. We have to build and rebuild new cities—the towering triangles of steel and titanium. We'll start with the museum! Think of how many buildings we could put in that space! All old things must be destroyed! Jettison the past!"

There was a centre of perfect blackness, like a drop of tar, in each of his eyes. Eric felt as if he were drowning in them. Chris, when is the tower going to overheat? he thought desperately. Why isn't it working?

"And Bob's going to spin for the bonus!" wailed a game-show host from one of the televisions. The studio audience sent up a huge groan.

Coyle's eyes flicked to the screen. "Don't do it, Bob!" he shouted. "You'll lose it all! Happens every time!"

Eric was startled by the intensity in Coyle's face. He was completely absorbed by the game show, his eyes locked to the television. Bob spun the wheel; the pointer missed the bonus mark and all his money was taken away from him by a beautiful woman. Coyle snorted in disgust.

"Protex laundry detergent," crooned another television, "is the detergent you've been dreaming about all these years."

"It's better than the leading brand!" Coyle chanted, snapping his gaze to the next screen. "Cleaner, faster, cheaper!"

"Don't leave me, Walter," pleaded a woman in a satin dress. "We can talk, we can work this out."

"Leave her, Walter!" raged Coyle. "She'll whine you deaf!"

Eric felt a chill pass through his body. It was as if Coyle had been mesmerized by the televisions. Symbols from the computer monitor swam across the ranting man's face, and as Eric watched, a green word wavered on his cheek.

WARNING.

155

Eric watched as it began to flash. Another message appeared across Coyle's mouth, distorted by the smile that was twisting his lips.

SYSTEM ERROR.

It's happening, Eric thought. Chris, it's working! He eyed the canister on the table. Should he make a run for it?

Coyle's gaze was fixed on another television screen. A bovine man dressed like Henry the Eighth was gorging himself on macaroni and cheese.

A horrible groan issued from the computer tower. Coyle whirled in alarm. One of the huge levers was grinding around laboriously. It faltered, turned a little more, then jammed. A jet of scalding oil shot from the machine's side.

"It's overheating!" Coyle hissed, looking down at his monitor. He saw the warnings, but before he could do anything, another message flared on the screen.

PURGING MEMORY.

"No!" Coyle shouted. "No!" His hands flew over the keyboard. Eric looked back to the memory tower. Wisps of smoke were lifting from its bristling mechanical surface. He saw Chris lean out from behind the base, flash the thumbs-up signal, and run for cover into the tangle of pipes and cables. They had shut it down, Eric thought jubilantly, but when he looked back at Coyle's computer monitor, the smile died on his lips.

EMERGENCY BACK-UP.
DOWNLOADING DATA TO MONITOR.

And then, before his amazed eyes, the translated contents of the live-forever machine began to scroll across the screen. His heart sank. They had been too late.

Coyle switched on the printer. A shriek rose from its insides and the machine went dead. "Come on!" Coyle growled, hitting buttons. "Work!"

The text was gradually filling the screen.

Coyle looked in a frenzy at his failing computer equipment. He knew he was going to lose the translation if he didn't hurry. His neon-blue eyes shone with terror. He grabbed a pen and a piece of paper. Eric watched as Coyle held the pen awkwardly, slowly forming his letters one at a time like a child. Eric couldn't believe it. So out of practice he'd almost forgotten how to write words.

The text of the live-forever machine had now filled the whole screen and was erasing itself as it scrolled. It was impossible for Coyle to keep up.

"You do it," he said, turning to Eric in pleading desperation.

Eric felt the slightest twinge of pity.

"Do it!" Coyle bellowed.

Eric shook his head, his knees trembling. Would he be shot?

But Coyle turned back to the screen and tried in vain to keep up. Now was the time. Eric snatched the canister and ran.

Chris emerged from their hiding place to meet him.

"It's done," Eric panted. "He's lost it." He looked back and saw Coyle still staring feverishly into the computer monitor. The screen suddenly exploded outwards, sending glass and sparks into his face. A horrible bellow rose from his throat.

"Back to the stairs," Chris said. And then they were

running, ducking and veering around hanging cables, hurdling over pipes. Eric had to push himself to keep up.

A sound like ripping fabric echoed through the concrete cavern, and a jagged spark flashed past them and arced down into the water.

"What was that?" said Chris.

"Lightning." Eric said breathlessly. He cast a glance over his shoulder and saw Coyle sprinting after them, the long rifle slamming against his ribs. His face was scored with glass cuts, oozing blood. "Just keep going! We'll outrun him."

Another spark shot past and struck a huge pipe. The pipe swayed slightly, and then the metal clamps holding it to the wall gave out, and it came crashing down across the cavern floor. Scalding steam filled the air. Eric raised a hand in front of his eyes and turned away, cursing. They'd never get through that.

He glanced at the water boiling through the storm drain. Too fast, too fast. He looked up. About five metres overhead, a pipe spanned the cavern.

"Up," Eric said to Chris. He found footholds in the wall. His hands grasped cables for support. Chris clambered up beside him, his useless gun clattering against the concrete and metal. They finally reached the pipe. It was thick enough to walk across, but it would be a tough balancing act. Coyle was gaining fast.

One foot darting in front of the other, Eric teetered across the pipe, afraid to slow down in case he lost his balance. The far wall slipped and shimmered before him.

"Hurry!" Chris shouted behind him.

"Stop!" Coyle roared. "You're very easy targets! I'm going to count to ten—no, let's make it backwards from five for novelty."

Eric could see their pursuer at the edge of the storm

drain, shouldering his lightning-maker. The glass cuts on his face had completely disappeared.

"Don't stop!" Eric called to Chris. "Keep going."

"Five ... four ..."

"We're not going to make it," Chris spluttered.

"Come on!"

"Three ..."

"Eric, we're not going to make it!"

"He won't do it! He needs the scroll!"

"Two ..."

"Eric—"

"One!"

Eric made it to the wall and looked wildly back over his shoulder. Chris was only about halfway across.

"Come on!" Eric yelled.

But Chris didn't move. Instead, he unslung the machine gun from his shoulder and, as Eric watched in horror, levelled it at Coyle, as if he were going to open fire. The air began to crackle with electricity.

Chris threw the gun into the air.

The bolt of lightning arched towards it and, in a flash, incinerated it. Eric looked back to Chris in relief, but his friend was swaying on the pipe, his arms flailing for balance.

"Chris!" Eric cried.

Another stroke of lightning slammed against the pipe and Chris fell forward, his hands grabbing air. Then it was all slow motion. Eric saw Chris's feet slip off the pipe. He saw his friend's mouth move, no sound, saw him hit the water below with a silent splash. And the current swept him away into the darkness.

Eric felt his throat constrict. Then his voice seemed to surge out of him.

"You bastard!" he screamed.

"The scroll!" Coyle wailed up at him. "I need the scroll."

"You killed him!" His mind had fogged with hatred.

"I'm promising you a glorious future, better than ever before, new and improved, bigger, faster, brighter. Don't you see the things I've been telling you?"

Eric looked at the trembling hand that clutched the canister, then down at the swirling water of the storm drain.

"You're running out of time!" shrieked Coyle. "I'm offering you the way of the future! Give me the scroll or I'll shoot!"

"I'll drop it!" he bawled back.

"No you won't," Coyle said with a sly smirk. "You're like old Alexander. You wouldn't ever do that."

Let it go, Eric commanded his fingers; just let it go.

"You won't do it," Coyle repeated.

Tears of frustration sprang up in Eric's eyes. Why couldn't he let it go? Come on! he raged inwardly. What does any of it matter now?

"You see," said Coyle. "You can't. Give it to me!"

And then Eric saw it: a glittering in the air in front of him, a bright sparkle.

Jonah's fishing hook.

In a single overhand swing of his arm, he plunged the canister's leather handle onto the hook and gave a sharp tug. And then the line was being reeled in and the scroll was drawn swiftly upwards.

And Eric started to laugh, a deranged laughter that he didn't even understand. It just tumbled out of his mouth, echoing against the walls of the cavern.

"No!" Coyle roared.

He heard the electric snap of the lightning-maker, and a spark hammered against a pipe next to his head. He pressed himself into the tangle of cables, tears streaming down his face. He could see Coyle on the far shore, waiting for his gun to charge up again.

"You've only wasted your own time," Coyle roared. "It's only a matter of years before I find the scroll again. I'll live forever!"

Eric was barely listening. He was moving fast towards a pipe that would shield him from the next blast.

"And do you know what else?" Coyle shrieked like an enraged child. "I'm going to make a fire like none you've ever seen! I'm going to burn the museum to the ground!"

A lightning bolt seared the wall and Eric was enveloped by smoke. Everything metal that he touched sent a shock through his fingers. The bitter smell of electricity clogged his nostrils.

"I'll raze it!" Coyle was shouting below. "I'm going to destroy it all."

"You can't!" Eric shouted back at him, hardly realizing what he was saying, forcing words through his burning throat.

"It can all be destroyed!" Coyle bellowed. "Like the rare-book library, like the antiques shop. Everything must be forgotten!"

He fired his rifle again and again. And then the air seemed to short-circuit and the lightning really started to fly, arching across the cavern with terrifying, sky-rending cracks.

"You can't destroy the past!" Eric shouted above the storm.

"I have!"

"You can't have forgotten it all. You're carrying it with you in your head!"

"No!"

"You can't get away from it!"

"I jettison the past!"

"The first electronic computer, 1942!"

"Shut up!"

"The first television, 1925!"

"No!"

"The first all-steel building, 1896!"

Horror seeped across Coyle's face.

"Henry Ford's first car, 1893!

"Ohm's Law, 1827!

"Benjamin Franklin's lightning conductor, 1752!

"Albrecht Dürer's flying machine, 1522!"

"Stop!" Coyle screeched.

"The Chinese use explosives, 1151!

"The birth of alchemy, 425!

"The fall of the Roman Empire, 400!

"The fire at the Library of Alexandria!"

Coyle shuddered and hunched forward convulsively, as if a huge weight had plummeted onto his shoulders.

"No!" he screamed. "No, it can't—"

Eric's hand touched something smooth and surprisingly cool. A wheel. The smoke cleared for a second and he could see a whole row of spoked wheels jutting out from the wall. The floodgates.

"You remember, don't you?" Eric screamed at him. "You remember it, Macer!" He bellowed out Coyle's real name.

Coyle convulsed again under the sudden, titanic rush of memory. "It's all got to be destroyed!" he shrieked in terror. "All of it! There's so much!"

Eric grabbed the first wheel with both hands and turned with all his strength, until it wouldn't turn any more. Then he moved to the next one.

"You'll never get rid of it all!" he wailed. "You can't ever forget it! There's thousands of years of it."

Eric turned another wheel. Then another and another.

"It's part of you, Macer. You *are* the past!"

Coyle's mouth was shaping words but Eric couldn't hear them. The immortal's whole body was trembling.

Then there was the sound of water. It was so loud, so sudden, that it seemed to drown out all the other noise. Then Eric saw it: water—more than a river, more than a lake, it must have been more than an entire ocean, he thought in that unreal moment as the waves came crashing down through the cavern, tumbling over the shores of the drain, sweeping over everything. He saw Coyle's computer tower topple under the massive waves, then the television sets and all the other machinery, gone, crushed beneath the powerful swell. Then he looked down at Coyle himself, standing absolutely rigid, watching the water rush towards him. Eric turned away and climbed as fast as he could, higher and higher, as the water rushed over his legs.

14

Fisher
of Men

Eric climbed blindly upwards, his thoughts roaring like TV static. His body was carrying him away from the rising water. The wall blurred before his eyes, shifting in and out of focus. His raw, bleeding hands grasped cables and metal clamps; his legs pumped against the solid bulk of pipes and concrete.

"Get back to the top!" he whimpered to himself, not knowing whether he was actually gasping out the words or they were just thudding around in his head. The surface. Get help, maps of the drains! He didn't want to come. He started to laugh again, but choked on it. You made him come. It's your fault. You forced him. You made him feel stupid all the time. He didn't want to come.

He paused, clinging to a pipe, his teeth gritted against the burning in his lungs. A quiet had descended over the flooded cavern. The tumultuous froth had calmed, and now only gentle ripples shimmered across the water's surface. He waited for more lightning, but it didn't come.

He began to climb again, more slowly now, resting often. But still his fragmented thoughts kept lurching out. Don't even know where the drain goes, where it empties out. Keep your head above water! Don't breathe it in! Where would you end up?

At last he hauled himself up onto a narrow catwalk and sprawled out on the damp metal. In his mind's eye he saw

Chris tumble into the rushing water before the cry had even fully escaped his lips. Without warning Eric's stomach and throat contracted. He retched once, twice—but there was nothing there.

Chris was dead. The truth came to him in a wave of nausea. The old things, all the dates—they weren't important. He'd been fooling himself. It was the people. That's what was important about the past. Had been all along, but he'd never seen it. It was the people who'd lived in those times, it was the people who'd made the old things. It was people living through history, creating an enormous chain with the people living now.

All those years memorizing dates and facts, and the real mystery was people. His mother, his father. That was what he'd wanted all along—to understand them. And Chris, too. But it was too late now. The answer was right in front of him and he'd lost it.

He pushed himself into a sitting position. He took deep breaths and felt his stomach slowly begin to uncoil. He stood. His legs wobbled beneath him and he touched the wall for balance. He had to get to the surface. If there was even the tiniest chance ...

He started walking unsteadily along the catwalk. The sound of water was a whisper below him now. He turned down a long tunnel. His sneakers slapped through the water pooled on the concrete floor. Rats darted from the shadows. He chose tunnels at random. His only rule was to climb every iron ladder, every set of steps. Eventually he had to break the surface of the city. He was falling asleep on his feet and dreaming. From the corner of his eye he saw a television set glowing at the end of a long corridor, a storm cloud of bats swooping towards him, an alligator's tail flick out of sight around a bend. Once he thought he saw Chris

and couldn't keep himself from calling out into the empti-
ness, staggering after the mirage.

"I'm sorry, I shouldn't ..." He was muttering, unable to
stop the words. "You didn't want to come. Dad, it's like a
maze down here. Were you really down here once? How
did you find your way out?"

A low-hanging cable struck him in the face, and he reeled
back in shock, whimpering uncontrollably. Dad, come and
get me, he pleaded silently. Right now, don't wait a second
longer.

He bit his lip to stop from crying, told himself to keep
moving. He had to tell someone about the accident, to get
help before all hope was lost. Half doubled over with
fatigue, he staggered along. Must look like Jonah, he
thought suddenly. Look and talk like Jonah.

"'... saw that the wickedness of man was great in the
earth, and that every imagination of the thoughts of his
heart was only evil continually ...'"

Eric paused and shook his head sharply from side to side.
Had he said that? He looked back over his shoulder, squinting down tunnel openings.

"'And the waters prevailed exceedingly upon the earth;
and all the high hills, that were under the whole heaven
were covered ...'"

It was definitely another voice.

"Alexander?" he said, his voice a dry crackle in his aching
throat. Suddenly dizzy, he slumped against the wall.
"Alexander? Is that you?"

"'... fifteen cubits upward did the waters prevail; and the
mountains were covered ...'"

Maybe Alexander would be able to help him find Chris;
maybe *he* would know about the drains, where they
emptied.

"Here!" he called out. "I'm right here!"

Where is he? Eric thought. Come on! But when he saw the silhouette moving towards him, he realized it wasn't Alexander. Too short and stocky.

" '...made a wind to pass over the earth, and the waters assuaged ...' " The figure was throwing his arms expressively out before him as he spoke. And there was another person. Two of them coming towards him.

Eric blinked, trying to keep his focus, but it was all dissolving before his eyes, seeping away from him.

" 'The fountains also of the deep and the windows of heaven were stopped, and the rain from heaven was restrained ...' "

He came to in a panic. Forcing himself up with his elbows, he looked wildly around. It was dark, and he was lying on an old inflatable mattress on the concrete floor. There were other people in the room, and a man was sitting beside him, watching him. Eric studied his face: it was the fire-and-brimstone preacher from the street corner. So that was who'd come for him in the tunnels.

He still felt as if his head were filled with sand, but at least he knew where he was. He could see the huge junk pile against the wall, and all the crazy contraptions the vagrants had made. Brushing the hair away from his forehead, he realized that his hands were bandaged. Burns, he thought. Burns from the hot pipes.

The fire-and-brimstone preacher was pressing a tin can into Eric's hands. Take it. He took a cautious sip—water—then drank greedily.

"Jonah," he said. "Is he here?" Maybe Jonah would know where to look for Chris.

The preacher shook his head.

"Got to go," Eric said, pushing himself into a sitting position. The man held him back, gently, but with surprising strength.

"I've really got to go," Eric said, feeling dizzy again. "My friend fell. Into the storm drain. Someone's got to know!"

"Wait here. You're too tired," the streetcorner preacher said, and Eric was surprised at the reasonable and calm voice. Eric was the only one who sounded crazy around here now!

"But you don't understand," he insisted. "Chris might be drowning!" He thought he was going to cry again. How could he ever explain this? Chris's mother, his own father? All Eric's fault.

"Whatever will happen has already happened," the preacher said soothingly. "Rest here."

Eric slumped back against the mattress. At the other side of the room, two of the underground people were building a couch, hammering together old planks and bits of broken furniture for the frame. Eric watched them blankly for a while. He had to get out of here.

He was about to get up when Jonah shambled in, carrying a plastic garbage bag over one shoulder and ranting about fish and rain and his biggest catch ever.

"Fisher of men!" he cried out triumphantly.

A second figure came into the room behind him, and in the low light Eric caught the glimmer of blond hair.

"Chris?"

He pushed himself to his feet before the preacher could reach out to hold him back. Soaked to the skin, looking slightly dazed, trying to towel that blond hair dry with one hand was Chris. Eric was across the room before Chris had recognized his voice.

"Oh, man, it's you!" Chris said. "I thought it was one of

these other guys trying to get me in a headlock!"

"How?" Eric demanded, still gripping Chris's shoulders and shaking him as if not quite convinced his friend was really there.

"It was hell down there," Chris said. "Backstroke for half an hour."

"What happened?"

"It was weird," Chris said, running a hand through his dripping hair. "I just got rushed through the drain, really fast—I couldn't really swim at all, just kept my head above water. Then the drain dumped out into this big reservoir, and I got squashed up against a net—can you believe it? A big fishing net stretched across the reservoir! Guess who?" He jerked his thumb in Jonah's direction. "It was utterly intense! And there were fish caught in it, too! So I kind of climbed along the net to the side and pulled myself out."

"Fisher of men," Eric said, and suddenly he was laughing, too happy and exhausted and relieved to stop.

"Yep," Chris said. "He showed me the way out. That place filled up like a tidal wave went through there. Hey, what happened to your hands?"

Eric looked down at the bandages, and then he began to tell Chris everything that had happened.

"You did it, then!" Chris said with a grin. "Coyle must've drowned. You did it!"

"What do you—?" Eric didn't understand.

"He *drowned*. If he drowns a second time he's unmade. Right?"

Eric hadn't even thought about it. There'd been too many other things clanging through his head. He nodded slowly. Ending someone's life, even someone insane and dangerous—it wasn't something you could be proud of. But they'd done it. They'd saved the museum. Still, it didn't seem

169

anywhere near as important as having Chris in front of him right now.

"Do you have it?" Chris was asking Jonah. "The scroll."

Jonah dropped his garbage bag to the ground with a soft thud. Sticking out the top was the tip of the white canister. He pulled it out and examined it in his hands.

"Strange fish," he said. He didn't seem to want to give it back, and Eric was tempted to let him have it. He'd keep it safely hidden away in his garbage bags forever. No one would ever know about it. And it was a dangerous thing, an unnatural thing. No one should live to be that old. But Eric knew he had to return it. He'd made a promise. He held out his hand, and Jonah reluctantly gave it back.

"Thanks," Eric said, and it suddenly occurred to him how much there really was to thank Jonah for—the hook, the fishing net—but Jonah didn't seem very interested. He had shuffled over to the junk heap and was rummaging through it. The streetcorner preacher was sitting against the wall, mumbling prayers.

"We should get out of here," Chris said. "It must be pretty late. Your Dad'll be worried."

Maybe, maybe not, thought Eric. He felt deflated. What would they have to say to each other? He looked back at the two people working on the couch. The billboard lady was weaving together old bits of clothing and fabric for the upholstery.

It was as if a key had suddenly opened a lock in his mind. Maybe that was something he could tell his father. He could tell him about the underground people and the way they saved up the old things so they could make new things out of them. Who knows, he thought—it might work, it might not. But it's worth a try.

Jonah nudged past Eric and began unpacking his plastic

bag, proudly throwing huge fish, one after the other, onto the floor.

"Come on," Chris said. "Let's get out of here before he asks us to stay for dinner."

Alexander snatched the canister and inspected the contents, wheezing heavily. Then he laughed—a dry, hollow croak. His eyes blazed.

"And Coyle," he said, looking back to Eric. "What of Coyle?"

"Gone," Eric said.

"Gone?" said Alexander, and there was an edge of alarm in his voice. "What do you mean? Tell me everything."

"We found Coyle. He was down there translating the scroll. He had a computer doing it for him, just the way Chris said he would." He felt sick telling it, and wanted to stop. He had to look away from Alexander's hungry eyes and force himself to continue. "We wrecked the computer and got the scroll and ran for it, but Coyle had some sort of gun that made lightning. The only way to get out was a pipe over the storm drain. Coyle took a shot at Chris and he fell into the water." He paused, sick. His friend, falling.

"Yes, yes, and then what?" Alexander said impatiently.

Eric looked at him with disgust. He really didn't care, did he? What would it mean to him anyway, someone dying? People came and went like insects.

"What else?" Alexander prompted him.

"I opened the floodgates. The water crashed over everything, his machinery, everything. Him, too."

"Did he drown?"

"He must have. It was like a tidal wave."

"You unmade him," Alexander said softly, disbelief in his voice.

"I wasn't really thinking," Eric replied. "It was the only way to stop him."

"To stop him—!" pressed Alexander. "To recover the scroll—that was your only task! You unmade him! Do you realize the magnitude of this?"

Eric stared in repulsion. "He was going to kill you," he said as calmly as possible. "And he was going to shoot me if I didn't give him the scroll, and would certainly have shot me anyway afterwards. He almost killed Chris."

But Alexander didn't seem to be listening. "He was more than sixteen hundred years old," he muttered. "He walked through history with me."

"You're crazy," Eric whispered. "He would have unmade you in a second!"

"You've wiped out two thousand years!"

"You're just as bad as Coyle," said Eric angrily. "All Coyle cared about was his machines and his future, and all you care about is your old things. Neither of you ever cared about anything else! Coyle was just another artifact to you, an old vase or statue. Chris almost *died*!"

"You have no understanding of what you're saying," Alexander mumbled, turning away. "At least now the museum is safe."

"If Chris had died," Eric shouted, "it wouldn't have been worth it at all!"

"You don't believe that," Alexander said with a smile.

Eric looked into his ancient eyes.

"Yes, I do."

Late evening. The plummeting raindrops made liquid

172

craters in the flooded street. A whirlpool sucked noisily above a storm drain grate. Cars had been left abandoned at the roadside. Eric took a deep breath, what felt like his first in days. Finally it was cooler. He'd showered at Chris's apartment and Chris had given him clean sweats to wear home. He'd carefully peeled the bandages off his hands. There were patches of red, blistered skin on his palms and across the backs of his fingers.

He took his time. He could see lights on in the living-room window. He pulled out his keys and opened the door. There was a nervous stirring in his stomach. What if nothing had changed? What if they still couldn't talk?

His father was sitting at the typewriter.

"Been out with Chris?" he asked.

"Yeah."

"I heard there was a gas leak here today."

"This morning. They closed it off, I guess."

His father looked back at the limp page curling out of the typewriter.

"Can't finish it," he said tiredly.

"It doesn't matter."

His father looked at him strangely. For a moment, Eric's courage faltered, but he knew it had to be now.

"Why did she do it? Kill herself?"

No answer. Eric felt a brief flash of fear: was his father going to get up and leave the room?

"I don't know," he said finally. "There were probably hundreds of reasons or none at all. I don't think I made her happy, or at least she wasn't happy with me."

Eric felt an overpowering urge to sweep away all the furniture and books in the room and start again.

"Maybe it didn't have anything to do with you," he said.

His father looked doubtful.

"Maybe it was just the way she was," he went on, "and no one could have helped her."

"She wasn't always unhappy. There were wonderful times. In Paris, for instance."

Dad was doing it again, travelling back, recreating conversations and scenes. Eric knew he had to break through the silence, but he wasn't sure how to begin.

"Would you do something for me?" he asked.

His father looked grieved. "What?"

"Write a story for me."

"Lots of stories upstairs. I'll give you any one of them."

"No, I don't want any of those. You wrote them for yourself."

"I suppose, but—"

"I want this one to be just for me. About her. Not made up. Tell me everything about her, all you knew."

"It would be a sad story."

"Will you do it?" It was the most important thing in the world that his father say yes.

"I don't know."

He watched his father stare at the typewriter. He reached out his hand and touched his father's forearm. He remembered how the dinosaur bone had felt in his grasp: cool, hard, lifeless. But this was warm and soft. This is the way you should hold onto people. With all your strength.

"It's been bad for you, hasn't it?" his father said, turning to him. "Not just me."

Eric nodded, awkward. "What about the story—"

"I'll try. I don't know how good it will be."

"You'll do it, though, right?"

"Yes."

"Promise."

"Yes. All right." Laughing awkwardly. "I promise."

"When?"

"Do you want me to start right now?"

"Tomorrow's fine. There's a story I want to tell you first."

THE END

Also available

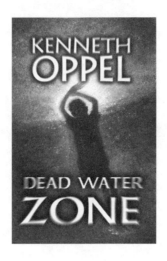

It's been months since Paul has seen his younger brother, Sam. Now Sam has disappeared.

Why?

The truth lies at the heart of Watertown, a polluted slum afloat in the city's toxic harbour, where Sam has been working as a research assistant. Paul goes there to find his brother – and encounters people who will do anything to stop him. Can Paul find out the truth? Or does the dead water zone devour everyone who dares to enter it?

An exciting thriller from the bestselling author of *Silverwing* and *Sunwing*, *Dead Water Zone* brings Kenneth Oppel's unique brand of gripping storytelling to an audience of older readers.